"THE KNIFE" STRIKES

"Kill them!" Roddy screamed to Morrell, and with his companion duplicating his action, he grabbed for his holstered revolver.

Two knives were brought from sheaths and were sent through the air with speed and precision. Thrown by a man who had been called *Cuchilo*—Knife—by the Comanche as a tribute to his skill in wielding that weapon, the massive James Black bowie passed between two of Roddy's ribs.

An instant later, directed with an equal accuracy, the clip point of the J. Russell & Co. "Green River" blade buried into Morrell. . . .

Books by J. T. Edson

THE NIGHTHAWK
NO FINGER ON THE TRIGGER
THE BAD BUNCH
SLIP GUN
TROUBLED RANGE
THE FASTEST GUN IN TEXAS
THE HIDE AND TALLOW MEN
THE JUSTICE OF COMPANY Z
McGRAW'S INHERITANCE
RAPIDO CLINT
COMANCHE
A MATTER OF HONOR
RENEGADE
WACO RIDES IN
BLOODY BORDER
ALVIN FOG, TEXAS RANGER
HELL IN THE PALO DURO
OLE DEVIL AT SAN JACINTO
GO BACK TO HELL
OLE DEVIL AND THE MULE TRAIN
VIRIDIAN'S TRAIL
OLE DEVIL AND THE CAPLOCKS
TO ARMS! TO ARMS, IN DIXIE!
TEXAS FURY
THE SOUTH WILL RISE AGAIN

Buffalo Are Coming!

J. T. EDSON

A DELL BOOK

Published by
Dell Publishing
a division of
Bantam Doubleday Dell Publishing Group, Inc.
1540 Broadway
New York, New York 10036

ISBN: 0-440-21046-1

Printed in the United States of America

Published simultaneously in Canada

June 1994

10 9 8 7 6 5 4 3 2 1

RAD

1

CAN IT BE DONE?

"Well, Captain Hart," Walter Johnson said, holding his normally carrying voice at a much lower pitch than usual as he had throughout the preceding conversation in order to emphasize he considered it of a most confidential nature. Always expressive, his florid and apparently jovial features implied great interest as he continued. "Everybody we've spoken to say you're the *best* trail boss there is. So may I ask you what you think of our idea?"

"For starters," answered the man to whom the question was directed, his accent that of a well-educated Texan and having a timbre of one capable of exerting authority, "I wouldn't want to come right on out and claim to be the *best* trail boss."

Regardless of the military honorific and protestation, even if failing to recognize him, anybody with a knowledge of the railroad and trail-end towns in Kansas could have deduced the speaker was actively involved with the major industry of the Lone Star State. A person with greater perception would also conclude he was something more than just a hired hand.

In his early thirties, six feet tall, Martin Jethro "Stone" Hart was clean shaven and had dark hair that was freshly barbered. Although he was no longer in the Army, he had been trained at West Point and had served with distinction, gaining the rank of captain, in Hood's Texas Brigade during the War Between the States. There was still much of the professional soldier's posture about his slender, yet clearly whipcord, tough frame. It suggested how his otherwise handsome tanned face had become disfigured by the livid white scar running the length of his right cheek. All his clean and good-quality attire—from the low-crowned, wide-brimmed brown hat dangling by its *barbiquejo* chin strap on the back of his chair, to the sharp-toed, high-heeled boots on his feet —was evidence of his connection with the cattle business, which had brought solvency back to Texas after the financial disruption caused by having seceded from the Union to become one of the Confederate States. Around his waist, a well-designed gun belt carried an ivory-handled Colt Civilian Model Peacemaker revolver in an open-topped holster clearly intended to permit its rapid withdrawal.

"I admire your modesty, my good sir!" Johnson asserted, his voice indicating he had been born and raised in Vermont, or some neighboring part of New England. "Nevertheless, that is the account of you we have had from everybody we questioned and, as I've told my associates, our project requires the best trail boss available. So, sir, we would like your opinion. Can it be done?"

Studying the big, bulky, well-dressed spokesman for the trio of obviously wealthy Easterners who had asked him to join them at a table in the Fair Lady Saloon, Stone Hart felt uneasy. Yet he was unable to decide exactly why this should be. A Yankee saber had marked him so badly that his fiancée had broken off their engagement on seeing the changed state of his face, and he had lost his home to carpetbaggers in the Reconstruction period following the war. However, neither event had given him an unreasoning hatred of Northerners. It was just that he had formed a vague dislike for the aura of bonhomie and eagerness to please him that exuded from Johnson. In a superior way, the attitude of the white-haired, distinguished-looking, fifty-or-so-year-old New Englander reminded him of a medicine show operator who employed a charming personality to peddle potions of dubious value to an unsuspecting population.

Being fair-minded, Stone was willing to concede that he found Johnson preferable to the other two occupants of their table.

In their mid-twenties, although Kevin Roddy was fair and Francis Morrell dark, physically they were much alike. Tall, thin, having hair longer than was considered acceptable by cowhands, their sallow and hollow-cheeked faces bore surly expressions as if disapproving of the company in which they found themselves. Despite being expensive, there was a slovenliness about their clothing that was voluntary rather than due to circumstances beyond their control. Neither had done more than given a brief acknowledgment on being introduced by Johnson, but the Texan had deduced they were the kind of well-to-do liberal intellectuals to whom all Southerners were anathema, and this had caused their close to standoffish behavior. On the other hand, they were also likely to be a party to the project—which he had to admit he found intriguing—described to him by their older companion.

"Nobody's ever tried anything like it," Stone said quietly.

"We know *that*!" Roddy exclaimed, his voice having the accent characteristic of an upper-class Bostonian. His manner implied he felt the conversation was getting nowhere, nor would it get anywhere.

"It's because nobody has done anything like it that we've come to *you*, sir," Johnson declared, after having directed a glare from which all bonhomie was removed at his fair-haired companion. "With the vast knowledge we've been assured you have acquired since forming your Wedge trail crew, we consider you're the man most likely to be able to tell us whether it would be possible."

"I've come to know more than a little about trail drives, I'll admit," Stone drawled. Unlike other Texans who brought longhorn cattle for sale to the railroad towns, he and his Wedge outfit were under contract to groups of ranchers who did not have sufficient stock individually to consider making the hazardous journey worthwhile. "But that's always been with cat—"

"What is it, sir?" Johnson inquired, as the explanation came to an abrupt end.

"This's a piece of luck," the trail boss commented, more to himself than the white-haired Easterner.

Turning his gaze in the direction Stone was looking, Johnson was puzzled. He found nothing about the four young men at present coming in a rough diamond-shaped formation through the main entrance to suggest why the comment had been made. One was an exceptionally fine figure and a second could be said to be striking in appearance, but they seemed little different from any of the other Texas cowhands to be seen around Mulrooney.

By virtue of his height being a good six feet three inches, having a tremendous spread to his shoulders, and a torso that trimmed to a slender waist set on long and powerful legs, the man at the right towered over his companions. Curly golden blond hair showed from beneath a white J. B. Stetson hat, molded in the style of Texas. His tanned features were almost classically handsome. All his clothing was made of the finest material and clearly tailored for him. Such an excellent fit could never have come straight from the shelves of a store. The brown *buscadero* gun belt he wore was carved with a basket-weave pattern, but the low-hanging ivory-handled Colt Cavalry Peacemakers were in fast-draw holsters and had clearly seen considerable use. Despite weighing over two hundred pounds, he gave no suggestion of being slow, clumsy, or awkward. Rather, he moved with a springiness that indicated a potential for very rapid motion when needed.

Lean and wiry, particularly in comparison with the golden blonde, the man on the left was about three inches shorter. Less costly, every item of it being black, his attire too was of the style practically *de rigueur* for a cowhand from Texas, except that his sharp-toed boots had low heels. His hair was so glossy black it seemed almost blue in some lights. Indian-dark, unless one looked carefully at his eyes—a curious red hazel color and giving a hint of a vastly different character—his features were babyishly handsome and seemed innocent. Regardless of this, at the right side of his gun belt a walnut-handled Colt Dragoon Model of 1848 revolver hung butt forward in a low cavalry-twist-draw holster. On the left was sheathed a massive ivory-handled James Black bowie knife.

Coming somewhere between the giant and the black-haired Texan in height and physique, being younger than both—the facial appearance of the latter notwithstanding—the cowhand bringing up the rear was another blonde, also good-looking. Apart from the addition of a brown and white calfskin vest, his garments were much the same as his companions'. Despite being only in his late teens, he wore his gun belt and twin staghorn Colt Artillery Model Peacemakers with assurance.

Compared with the other three, including the blond

youngster, the leading Texan seemed insignificant and practicially diminutive. Not more than five feet six in height, aided by the high heels of his cowhand-style footwear, his tanned face was no more than moderately good-looking and far from eye-catching. Tilted back on his head, his black hat displayed dusty-blond hair. Knotted about his throat, the long ends of a tightly rolled scarlet silk bandana trailed over the front of an open-necked dark green shirt. Hanging outside his tan-colored boots, the legs of his blue jeans had been turned up to form cuffs almost three inches deep. Although his clothes were as costly as those worn by his companions, somehow he contrived to give them the air of having been handed down to him as somebody else's castoffs. Not even a well-made gun belt, with two bone-handled Colt Civilian Model Peacemakers in cross-draw holsters, served to make him any more noticeable, especially in the company he was keeping.

"It seems you're known to them, Captain Hart," Johnson remarked, watching the shortest blonde raise a hand in a gesture of greeting and start to walk toward the trail boss, followed by the other three. Wondering why they were allowing themselves to be led by such a diminutive person, he went on, "Or perhaps they are more members of your crew?"

"They're not, it's Du—" Stone commenced, but once again he was distracted before he could finish a comment. "Damn it, won't those two red-topped yahoos *ever* learn?"

The New Englander turned his gaze, as he had previously, to ascertain what was attracting the trail boss.

On arriving at the Fair Lady Saloon, where he had been told he could locate the man he was seeking, Johnson had found Stone sitting at a table on the right of the front entrance with several members of the Wedge trail crew. Two of them, with different shades of red hair, were now leaving

their chairs. While listening to their conversation from outside the batwing doors, prior to entering and asking the trail
boss for a few minutes' private conversation, the New Englander had heard the taller and more fiery-haired cowhand
called "Johnny" and the other referred to appropriately as
"Rusty."

Waiting until the four newcomers had gone by their table,
the redheads exchanged comments briefly and followed.
Passing swiftly on either side of the blond giant and the
black-dressed Texan, they lunged inward. Showing what
might have been considered commendable teamwork under
different circumstances, Johnny grabbed the small cowhand
by the left wrist and back of the dark green shirt collar. At
the same moment, Rusty caught hold of him in the same
fashion from the right. Having done so, they began to hustle
him in a half circle away from his companions.

"We're not having no Rio Hondo varmints any place we
are!" Johnny announced, without so much as a precautionary glance at the three Texans accompanying the small man
they were grasping. "Are we, Rusty?"

"We for sure ain't!" seconded the other Wedge cowhand,
paying just as little attention to what most people would
have considered a potential and potent source of objection
to their behavior. "Outside's the place for such!"

Seeing his young companions were exchanging startled
and worried glances, and possessing a far greater experience
of such matters, Johnson was prey to even greater misgivings. It had been several years since he had spent time west
of the Mississippi River, but his earlier dealings with cowhands from the Lone Star State had taught him how the
majority had considerable pride in, and loyalty for, the ranch
by which they were hired. On entering the saloon, he had
noticed that four separate groups of Texans were present as
well as customers from other Western occupations. All were

watching with an interest he found disturbing. He was familiar with how quickly a full-scale brawl could develop among
such a crowd should they become aroused. What was more,
once the fighting commenced, even those occupants of the
barroom who had no desire to become involved might be
attacked before they could state their specific intentions.

Even as the New Englander was drawing his unpalatable
conclusions over the events taking place near the main entrance, he became aware that there was something puzzling
about certain responses being shown to them.

Despite members of the Wedge crew behaving in a most
untoward fashion, Stone Hart was giving no indication of
concern or rising to intervene!

On returning his gaze to the other three newcomers,
Johnson discovered to his surprise that they too were displaying a remarkable disinterest!

Instead of offering to help their companion, the blond
giant looked at the other two and gave an almost Gallic
shrug of his shoulders. Glancing at the men holding the
small cowhand, the youngster—whom the New Englander
would have expected to take some form of action no matter
what was done by his companions—did nothing more than
give a shake of his head redolent of sympathy for an error
being committed. Then all three continued to stroll toward
the counter as if nothing untoward was taking place behind
them.

Before Johnson could ponder upon the reaction of the
trail boss and the other three new arrivals, which struck him
as being peculiar to say the least, his attention was again
diverted!

Neither speaking nor attempting to struggle against the
grips of his captors, the small cowhand appeared to have
accepted his eviction as inevitable!

Allowing himself to be forced away from his apparently

disinterested companions, seeming even more diminutive in comparison with even the shorter of his assailants, the blonde began to move his feet after the fashion of a soldier changing step to conform with the rest of a parade. Having achieved the requisite step, he braced his weight suddenly upon his stiffened left leg. Raising the right, bending it at the knee, he brought its thigh parallel to the floor. Inclining his torso forward, being helped to retain his balance by pulling against the hands that were grasping him, he snapped the elevated limb backward. Guided with accuracy, regardless of his being unable to look where it was going, the edge of the tan-colored boot's instep struck Rusty just below the left knee. Letting out a startled and pain-filled yelp, the powerfully built, ruggedly good-looking trail hand released his hold and staggered back a few steps.

On effecting the escape from the clutches of his shorter assailant, the small blonde brought the foot that did this down to his right rear. To Johnson, it seemed he was making a mistake. The movement caused his left hand to be twisted behind his back. However, he immediately raised the liberated arm in front of his chest until its clenched fist was almost touching his left shoulder. Then, rotating his hips vigorously to the right, he chopped his elbow around. Striking Johnny in the midsection with considerable power, it elicited a spluttering grunt and, forced to let go of the wrist and collar, he too stumbled away.

Before the small blonde could do any more, Rusty returned to the fray. Jumping forward, he encircled the newcomer's arms from the rear in a bear hug. Eager to make the most of this, Johnny lunged forward with eagerly reaching hands. Once more, the diminutive intended victim proved equal to the needs of the situation. Making no attempt to escape from the arms that were pinioning his own to his sides, he shifted his weight onto his right leg and bent it slightly at the knee. Then he brought up and shot out his left foot with great rapidity. Walking into the rising boot, which took him in the pit of the stomach, the fiery-haired Wedge rider gave vent to another agonized squawk. Folding at the waist, his advance was turned into a hurried retreat. Nor did his misfortunes end there.

Having delivered the kick, the blonde swiftly lowered his foot so it passed between the spread-apart legs of the man to his rear. While doing so, he pivoted his lower torso to the left and began to spread his arms apart with an upward surging motion. Small he might be, but he clearly was far from being puny. Although his actions did not break the bear hug completely, they caused it to be loosened sufficiently for his purposes. Reversing the direction taken by his hips, he propelled his left elbow against the solar plexus of the man to his rear.

Despite the blow having traveled only a short distance and from a less than advantageous position, it proved most effective. Breath belched from Rusty and his arms fell apart from their captive. As he reeled backward, he began to tilt at the middle like a jackknife being closed. Before he could pass beyond reaching distance, the blonde spun to catch him by the right wrist and biceps. Turning rapidly on his left heel, giving further evidence of his surprising strength, he sent his former captor hurtling around. Released at the appropriate moment, Rusty rushed in a headlong collision with the still bent over Johnny, which sent them both to the floor in a tangled pile.

Fascinated by what he was watching, Johnson became aware that somebody else was about to participate.

Unnoticed by the New Englander until that moment, the owner of the Fair Lady Saloon was striding purposefully across the barroom toward the three Texans.

In spite of her sex and the fact that she lived in what was

still basically a "man's world," Freddie Woods was unique in more ways than one. Not only did she operate the finest establishment of its kind in Mulrooney, but she was also the mayor and was credited with forming the policies that made it considered by visitors the most honest and fair dealing of the Kansas railroad and trail-end towns.

No more than in her mid-twenties, Freddie was a fine figure of a woman. Five feet eight in height, with immaculately coiffured raven-black hair topping a regally beautiful face, she would have caused masculine heads to turn in any company. Such were the magnificent curves of her close to "hourglass" figure, she contrived to make the sober black two-piece costume and white blouse she had on seem as revealing as the most daring evening gown. Nevertheless, her expression and demeanor suggested to the New Englander that she was a person with whom it would be ill-advised to take liberties, or to trifle. He also deduced it was her intention to deal with the trouble causers.

"You *bully*!" the beautiful young woman announced, coming to a halt between the Texans and placing her hands on hips. Her accent was that of the British upper class. "How dare you pick on and abuse those poor boys?"

The question came as much of a surprise and puzzle to Johnson as had the behavior of Stone Hart and the blonde's three companions!

On coming to a halt, Freddie had her back to Johnny and Rusty!

Furthermore, the words were directed at the small cowhand!

2

OUR BUSINESS IS MOST
CONFIDENTIAL

"You rawhide that Rio Hondo varmint real good, Miz Freddie, ma'am!" Jason "Rusty" Willis requested somewhat breathlessly, rolling clear of the other Wedge rider and thrusting himself slowly into a sitting position on the floor.

"Why sure, seeing's how he's allus picking on poor defenseless lil ole country boys like us," supported Jonathan Edwin "Johnny" Raybold, also having to replenish lungs in need of air and showing just as little surprise over the attitude adopted by the owner of the Fair Lady Saloon. He too hoisted himself laboriously into a seated posture and continued hopefully, "You hand him his needings, Miz Freddie, 'n' we'll be right *behind* you while you're doing it."

Suiting the deed to the word, conveying the impression that they were two small boys seeking the protective shield offered by their mother's skirt, the two red-haired cowhands scrambled to their feet and remained so that the beautiful

Englishwoman was between them and the man they had attacked.

"I just *knew* you could be counted upon to do that," Freddie Woods declared, looking over her shoulder as if approving of what the pair were doing. Then, although her words continued to be intended for them, she swung a less indulgent gaze toward the small Texan. "Go back and sit with your friends, you poor dear boys. I'll have one of my young ladies bring you the drink I'm *sure* this dreadful *bully* is going to buy for each of you."

"Why *gracias*, Miz Freddie, you're a for real kind 'n' generous lady," Johnny thanked fulsomely. "Which 'most everybody here'd say all truthful true's how we deserve nothing *less*, what he did to us."

"I just knowed's we could count on *you* to see the right thing was done by us, ma'am," Rusty asserted, contriving to sound just as unctuous as his fiery-haired companion. "What say's we go get the drinks that there *bully's* going to be made buy us, huh, *amigo*?"

"That's right," the Englishwoman smiled. "You trot along like good little boys and I'll deal with the bully for you."

"Whew!" Walter Johnson exclaimed, as the redheads went to rejoin the rest of the Wedge crew at their table. Watching Freddie approaching the small Texan, regardless of how she had spoken, he could see no trace of animosity in her demeanor. In fact, he considered her greeting held a warmth that went far beyond that of a saloonkeeper dealing with an ordinary good—or even influential—customer. "I thought there was going to be *trouble*!"

"Shucks, no," Stone Hart replied, having sensed his passive acceptance of the situation was puzzling the New Englander. "It always happens that way."

"You mean this isn't the first time your men have attacked that little man?" Johnson gasped.

"Not the first, nor likely to be the last if I know those two knob-heads of mine," the trail boss confirmed. "Ever since they saw Dusty using some of those fancy wrestling tricks he's learned from General Hardin's Japanese servant, they've been taken by the notion that they can get the better of him." Pausing and shaking his head as if unable to credit such folly, he concluded, "They never have, though. And I'll be surprised if they ever will."

"I thought it was strange when you just sat here instead of doing anything to stop them," the New Englander admitted.

"Hell, I knew it was all in fun and he wouldn't hurt them," Stone answered, then raised his voice. "Hey, Dusty. Can you spare a couple of minutes for me, please?"

"Why sure, *amigo*," the small blonde agreed, ending what had been closer to holding than just shaking the hand of the beautiful Englishwoman. "Will you excuse me, please, Freddie?"

"Of course, *bully*," the saloonkeeper assented. "Just so long as you don't try to use it as an excuse to forget you owe me for the drinks for those two poor boys you were picking on."

"I heard you were in town, Stone," the blonde greeted, on arriving at the table. "It's good to see you, even if you did get *lucky* and beat us here."

"I'd like to see the day when the Wedge can't beat you OD Connected bunch to *anything*, up to and including long-distance spitting against the wind," the trail boss claimed, but without rancor, exchanging a handshake indicative of mutual respect and friendship. Looking at the Easterners, he went on, "Gentlemen, allow me to present Captain Dustine Edward Marsden Fog."

"My pleas—" Johnson commenced instinctively, but without warmth. Then, realizing the import of the name he had heard, he stared at the blonde as if unwilling to accept the evidence of his eyes and he gasped, *"Dusty Fog?"*

"Dusty Fog," Stone confirmed, smiling despite noticing how Kevin Roddy and Francis Morrell were eyeing the small Texan with obvious disfavor. Deciding against going further in the matter of introductions, he continued, "I'd like your opinion on something these gents have—"

"Excuse me, Captain Hart and with no offense intended to you, Captain Fog," the white-haired New Englander interrupted, his manner polite yet prohibitive. "Our business is most *confidential.*"

"I know it is and you can count on Dusty to keep it that way," the trail boss of the Wedge claimed. "Only what you've asked me is so *unusual* and out of the ordinary, I'd like to hear what he thinks about it."

Aware that his two young companions were moving restlessly and feeling sure neither would be in favor of the decision he was about to make, Johnson did not offer to consult them.

A keen judge of character, the New Englander had been studying the man called to the table even before hearing his name. Being able to see beyond external appearances, or mere feet and inches of height, Johnson had assessed the true potential of the small Texan. He had a muscular development that was not apparent at first sight, yet explained how he was able to cope with two larger and heavier assailants. What was more, there was a strength of will and intelligence about the tanned young face, and the gray eyes held the undefinable look of one possessing the inborn ability for commanding obedience that characterized a natural leader.

Having reached his conclusions, the New Englander was willing to concede that there could be justification for all the stories he had heard about Dusty Fog!

"As you wish, Captain Hart, as you wish," Johnson assented, after throwing a look of prohibition at his associates, who were both clearly on the point of registering a protest. Waiting until they had sunk back on their chairs, scowling balefully, he went on, "But I must ask you to give me your word not to disclose *anything* of what you hear to *anybody*, Captain Fog."

"You have it," the small Texan promised and took the chair indicated by the New Englander.

"This is Mr. Johnson, Mr. Roddy, and Mr. Morrell, Dusty," Stone introduced, but only the first man he named offered to shake hands with the blonde. Concluding the behavior of the other two stemmed from a resentment of the reputation acquired by his *amigo* while serving with great success in the Texas Light Cavalry against the Union during the War Between the States, he elected to ignore them. "They represent the Society for the Preservation of the American Bison. Happen you've heard of it?"

"I've read something about it in newspapers Uncle Devil's had sent by friends back east," Dusty admitted. "You're aiming to save the buffalo from being wiped out."

"And *you* don't agree with that," Roddy stated, rather than asked.

"You must excuse my young friend, Captain Fog," Johnson put in, directing a baleful glower at the fair-haired young Easterner. "But he feels very strongly about the aims of the Society."

"Uh huh!" the small Texan grunted noncommittally. Having formed similar conclusions regarding the political aspirations of Roddy and Morrell to those of Stone Hart, he was in no way surprised nor put out by their unconcealed animosity. However, bearing it in mind, he directed his next words more to the older New Englander than them. "Living out here and being in the ranching business, I don't see how the herds of buffalo could've been let stay as large as they used to be. But I for sure wouldn't want to see every last one of them wiped off the face of the earth. That'd be more than just wasteful, it'd be a sin."

"Good for you, sir, and well said!" Johnson praised, although his sullen-faced companions showed no such indication of being impressed or rendered more amiable by what they had heard. "And those are the sentiments of the Society." Then, remembering how the blonde had learned of the organization, he considered it was advisable to add, "Of course, I can't deny there are those among our membership who talk of restoring the bison to their former vast numbers. However, the *majority* of us are more practical. We realize this isn't possible, desirable as doing so might appear. With an ever-growing flow of immigrants from Europe arriving in search of new homes and the West being opened up for settlement, we accept there can be no place for millions of large wild animals to roam unchecked and in competition with domestic stock for grazing. No, sir. The aim of our Society is merely to ensure a viable breeding population of bison is maintained for the benefit of future generations."

"You won't get any argument from me on doing that," Dusty declared and, despite having the dislike of a man of action for such professionally delivered rhetoric, he was impressed by the apparent sincerity of the distinguished-looking New Englander. "Fact being, you'll have the full backing of General Hardin in doing it."

"That will be most gratifying," Johnson asserted. "The more men of the General's influence we can gather to our cause, the greater chance of it succeeding. However, the matter that brought us here is still of a most delicate and confidential nature . . ."

"I understand!" the small Texan confirmed, as the New Englander let the words trail to an end accompanied by a significant stare. "And I won't mention it, even to the General, unless you've said it will be all right for me to do so."

"That satisfies *me*, sir!" Johnson replied, once more staring in a mixture of defiance and prohibition at his companions. "Our purpose of coming west, sir, will, I feel sure, be of considerable interest to you."

"What they have in mind, Dusty," Stone Hart supplied, when the New Englander once more stopped speaking, being determined that the blonde should not have to ask for an explanation, "is to get a herd of a thousand or more buffalo driven to a section of range they've bought, so's to make sure there'll be a fair few left to breed should all the rest be wiped out by skin hunters and such."

"That's a right smart notion," Dusty said quietly, thinking of the difficulty in implementing such a venture.

"Thinking of having it done is the *easy* part, as you've clearly realized, Captain Fog," Johnson remarked. "Particularly as, while our Society holds sufficient funds to pay for the project, none of us possesses either the knowledge or the skill to carry it out. That is why I—my associates and I"—the amendment was made due to the two younger Easterners moving restlessly on hearing him apparently taking full credit without including them—"have come to Mulrooney. We believed that we could find a man here who can tell us, from practical experience, whether it could be done."

"You've come to the right man with Stone here," the small Texan claimed. "Excepting for Colonel Goodnight, I'd say there's *nobody* knows more about trail herding than he does."

"Easy there, *amigo*, you'll be making me blush," the scar-faced trail boss warned, trying to prevent himself showing the pleasure he felt at the compliment. "And you're no slouch at handling a bunch of cattle yourself. That's why I asked you over. Do *you* reckon it can be done?"

"I don't know and that's the living truth," Dusty confessed, but he obviously found the subject of great interest. "I know buffalo are like cattle in a lot of ways. Fact being, Uncle Charlie's often talked about trying to cross buffalo with longhorns although he hasn't got around to doing it yet. But, so far as I know, nobody's ever tried driving a herd of buffalo from place to place, much less holding them on a particular piece of range to breed and live like they was cattle."

"No white man's tried driving them, anyways," Stone supplemented, glancing in a pointed fashion to where the three cowhands who had entered with the small Texan were standing at the bar talking to Freddie Woods and a few of her girls. "But maybe the Indians have."

"Lon would likely know if they have," Dusty commented, guessing what the trail boss had in mind. "He's one of my *amigos,* Mr. Johnson. Can I call him over and ask?"

"Good God!" Morrell yelped, his East Coast accent high-pitched and petulant in timbre. "Just how many *more* of these pec—people are we expected to tell what we're wanting to do?"

"Lon's part Indian, Mr. Johnson," Stone put in, making it plain he considered the decision lay with the white-haired New Englander. "He can maybe tell you whether any of them ever tried herding buffalo and, should we bring him in on the deal, you can count upon his discretion just as much as you can Dusty or me."

"Certainly not!" Roddy claimed, and Morrell commenced a similar protest. "It's out of the quest—"

"Just one moment, *gentlemen!*" Johnson snapped, employing a vehemence that brought the words of the two young Easterners to a halt. "When I agreed to come out here with you, it was on the clear understanding that I was to be in charge of all the negotiations for yo—*the Society's* project. Isn't that so?"

"Yes!" Roddy admitted, after a brief period of sullen scowling.

"It is!" Morrell concurred, with no better grace, on being subjected to a cold and challenging glare by the grim-faced New Englander.

"Very well, then, my decision is that we allow Captains Hart and Fog to do as they think best," Johnson declared and, looking at Dusty, lost the belligerence from his voice. "Call your man over, sir, if you consider he can be of assistance to us."

"Lon!" the small Texan obliged. "You stop telling lies about me to Freddie and head on across here!"

"Yo!" responded the summoned member of the trio with the beautiful Englishwoman, giving the traditional assent to an order of the United States' cavalry.

Subjecting the black-dressed Texan to a careful scrutiny as he was approaching, Johnson concluded that—like the small blonde—he was much more than appeared at first sight. Certainly he was somewhat older and far less babyishly innocent than was implied, unless one noticed and took into account his red hazel eyes and his Indian-dark features. He would, in fact (his apparently old fashioned armament notwithstanding), prove a very bad man to cross. Even when strolling peacefully in a leisurely fashion across the barroom, there was an underlying controlled menace to his every movement. He gave a suggestion, much as did a cougar ambling along, that he could erupt into sudden and deadly motion should the need arise.

"For shame, *amigo*!" the newcomer protested, his accent indicating origins in a less affluent section of the Lone Star State's society than the other two Texans at the table. It also had a pleasant tenor timbre that suggested he might be a good singer. "Now would I *lie* about *anything*?"

"Was you to tell me that Monday comes a day before Tuesday every week, I'd go straight out and check a calendar," Dusty claimed. "Gentlemen, with my sincere apologies for bringing him into your company, let me present the Ysabel Kid."

"I assumed you would be he, sir," Johnson asserted truthfully, deciding that here was another man who would live up to much of what was told about him. He also noticed how, although neither had offered to do so when introduced to Stone Hart and Dusty Fog, his companions were rising and extending their right hands to the black-clad Texan. "Have a seat, sir, please."

"Gracias," the Kid answered, drawing out a chair after he had shaken hands with the young Easterners.

"By gad, this is remiss of me, Captain Fog!" the New Englander boomed. "Perhaps you and Mr. Ysabel would like a drink?"

"Just a beer will do for me, please," Dusty accepted.

"The same for me," agreed the black-dressed Texan, sitting down.

3

THEY CAN'T TALK IF THEY'RE *DEAD*

"Well, sir," Walter Johnson said, after the drinks had been delivered and he had explained to the latest arrival at the table something of the project that the Society for the Preservation of the American Bison had concocted. "Did you ever see, or hear of, bis—*buffalo* being driven?"

"I've never done it myself, nor even seen it done," the Ysabel Kid answered. "But Grandpappy Long Walker told me's how you could get a big bunch of 'em to head the way you want, if you do it slow and easy."

"How big a bunch?" the New Englander inquired.

"He allowed to have helped haze along over a thousand head at a go in his day," the black-dressed Texan replied.

"Ah yes!" Kevin Roddy put in, with the air of one who considered he was stating the obvious. "That would be so they could select and kill only the most suitable animals, then release the rest, of course."

"Select and release *nothing*!" the Kid corrected. Duplicating the summations of his fellow Texans, he also sensed that where he was concerned the attitude of the young Easterners was governed by knowing he had mixed blood, and he had no liking for the somewhat condescending friendliness to which they had treated him on being introduced. "The idea was to get the whole bunch of 'em to where they could all be stampeded over a cliff together."

"But *nothing* was wasted," Morrell asserted. "Not as it is these days!"

"Like hell nothing was wasted," the Indian-dark Texan denied, thinking how people of the young Easterners' outlook and persuasions always sought to show in a favorable light any race they considered to be acceptable underdogs. "They'd take no more than they wanted and leave all the rest for the coyotes and buzzards, just like white folks do. Fact being, if they picked wrong and the bunch went over a cliff where it'd be hard work fetching out the hide 'n' meat, they'd leave 'em all to rot and go find another bunch for driving."

"I feel we're straying from the point, gentlemen!" Johnson injected firmly. Knowing his companions were completely lacking in tact when any of their beliefs were questioned, he silenced them with a glare before either could continue the discussion. "The thing that interests me most is, could just any Indian do the driving?"

"Not when it came to moving the herd to where it was wanted," the Kid supplied, the question having been directed at him. "Only braves who'd been taught 'specially could do that."

"Uh huh!" the New Englander grunted, nodding as if to indicate he had expected to hear what he had been told. "And would such drive be for a long distance?"

"No further than could be helped," the black-clad Texan

answered. "They wouldn't be kept moving for more than half a day at most."

"Unless I'm reading the sign wrong," Stone Hart drawled, "I'd guess you'll be figuring on moving your herd a whole heap further than that."

"We are, sir, we are indeed," Johnson confirmed. His tone took on a suggestion of making a statement, rather than delivering a query, as he continued, "So doing it will be a job for experts?"

"If you tried it without fellers's knowed *everything* about what they was doing and could do it," the Kid claimed, "you'd wind up with the herd scattered to hell 'n' gone the first time any lil thing at all went wrong. Which said, sure's sin's for sale in Cowtown, things'd start going wrong 'most straightaway."

"It wouldn't be *easy,* even with a well-trained crew," Dusty Fog estimated. "Buffalo might live in herds like cattle and eat the same kind of food, but they're not even partly domesticated like longhorns."

"And longhorns can be hell to handle, even for men who've grown up around them," the trail boss of the Wedge supplemented. "So I don't know whether buffalo could be driven like them, but it'd make a mighty *interesting* challenge to find out."

"It would indeed, sir, it would indeed!" the New Englander agreed. "However, unless they feel they have any more to add, I feel we've imposed for quite long enough upon Captain Fog's and Mr. Ysabel's time and, with our thanks, they can rejoin Miss Woods and their companions."

"Stone can tell you more than either of us about whatever else you'll need to know now," Dusty asserted, accepting what had amounted to a dismissal and shoving back his chair. "Which being, the sooner I go stop those other two knob-heads blackening my good name with Freddie, the happier I'll feel."

"We're grateful to you both for having given so freely of your time and advice," Johnson declared, rising and extending his right hand toward the small Texan. Neither of his companions offered to duplicate his action, either to Dusty or the Kid, so he went on, "You will, of course, impress upon Mr. Ysabel the importance of keeping what we've been discussing confidential, Captain Fog. Having it become known that we're planning to move and settle so many buffalo would arouse a storm of protest in some quarters, and there will be others who'll consider it a God-sent opportunity to hunt down the unfortunate beasts, as is being done everywhere else they still exist."

"You can count on us not to say a word about it to *anybody*," Dusty promised, and the Kid nodded his concurrence. "And we both wish you all the best of luck with what you're hoping to do."

* * *

"Damn it all!" Francis Morrell protested, his high-pitched voice quivering with petulant indignation. "Why do we need to spend our money on having that God damned peckerwood Hart and his lousy redneck hired hands to drive the bison for us?"

"Because, brilliant as you may consider yourselves, none of you has either the knowledge or the experience to even start doing it," Walter Johnson replied, showing not the slightest concern over being subjected to six stares varying from disapproving to frankly hostile. "I doubt whether any of you, white or red, could be counted on to even sit a horse well enough to start the herd moving, much less cope with any of the emergencies that are sure to arise."

After Dusty Fog and the Ysabel Kid had left the table at the Fair Lady Saloon, the New Englander had got down to the business that had brought him to Mulrooney. As was anticipated by Stone Hart, despite the obvious disapproval of the two younger Easterners, Johnson had negotiated on behalf of their Society to obtain the services of the Wedge crew for the proposed transfer of the buffalo. Quoting a price that more than satisfied the trail boss, he warned this carried the proviso of being willing to work under what—in shipping circles—would have been termed "sealed orders" with regard to the final destination. Using the same reasons he had given for insisting that the two members of the OD Connected ranch should refrain from mentioning the project, even to their closest associates, he had stressed the vital necessity for everything to do with it being kept a secret. Agreeing the precaution was justified, Stone had accepted the terms and declared his men would be willing to accompany him without knowing more than that they had a herd of some kind to deliver.

With the matter concluded, clearly in a manner less to the satisfaction of Kevin Roddy and Morrell than for the two negotiators, the meeting had been concluded. Arranging to meet Johnson for further discussions upon what would be needed for the drive, the trail boss had rejoined his crew. Leaving the saloon, the Eastern trio did not return to the rooms they were occupying at the expensive and luxurious Railroad House Hotel. Instead, they had made their way through a lower-rent district to the smaller and less costly establishment in which four more members of their party had found accommodation to lessen the chance of their being connected with one another.

Faced by the quartet on arrival, in spite of their soberly colored city clothing being of a better quality than was the norm for intended guests, the desk clerk at the Grimsdyke Temperance Hotel had been dubious about allowing them to rent rooms. They had been different in other ways from the

usual kind of visitors who came his way. In their mid-
twenties, of different heights and builds, they had either
aquiline or slightly Mongoloid coppery-brown faces that reminded him of paintings he had seen depicting various kinds
of Red Indians. However, while their hair was black and
rather longer than would have been permitted by cowhands,
it did not extend to shoulder level as he had heard was
generally the case with braves. What was more, they had all
spoken excellent English with no trace of a "foreign" accent.

Guessing what was worrying the clerk, one of the four had
explained their alien appearance by claiming they were recent immigrants from Bohemia. Although uncertain of the
country's exact location, the clerk had a vague recollection it
was somewhere in Eastern Europe. Therefore, when it was
suggested by the spokesman that they pay for their rooms in
advance, he had put aside his misgivings and opened the
register, which they signed with the appropriate-sounding
names "Ivan Boski, Peter Romanov, Rudolph Petrovich, and
Hugo Budapest." Nor had he been given any cause to regret
the decision to accommodate them. They had kept to themselves and behaved in a more decorous fashion than was
occasionally the case with more conventional guests.

Morrell joined the quartet in the room occupied by
"Boski" and "Petrovich." He raised a protest when Johnson
described what had taken place at the Fair Lady Saloon.

The answer from the New Englander did not go unchal-
lenged!

"You don't have to include all of *us*!" stated the shortest,
most thickset and Mongoloid-looking of the four, who had
signed the register "Hugo Budapest." "We Osage have always been excellent horsemen!"

"Not *always,* only since you caught horses that were
brought over here by the Spaniards and escaped," Johnson

corrected dryly. "And, in any case, you've never been near one since you were sent east as a boy."

"That's true enough!" agreed tall, slender, and hawk-faced "Peter Romanov," with a mocking grin.

"I know more about riding than *you,* anyway!" "Buda-pest" claimed heatedly. "No Yakima seed-gatherer ever took the war trail, or even walk—"

"At least we *never* became lickspittle runarounds for the Army!" "Romanov" countered. "Which is more than can be said for the Os—"

"Debating tribal differences won't change *anything*!" Johnson interrupted firmly, stepping between the two clearly angry younger men. "*We* can't drive the buff—*bison,* if you insist—ourselves. So you'll have to accept it must be done by somebody who can!"

"But why does it have to be a bunch of lousy Southern peckerwood scum who fought against us during the Rebellion?" demanded Roddy sullenly.

"Because *Captain* Hart and his Wedge crew are the best there is," the New Englander replied, unable to resist the temptation to annoy the fair-haired Easterner by employing the military honorific. However, he decided to refrain from pointing out that the other had done no fighting whatsoever in the War Between the States. "Certainly they're the best available who aren't attached to a particular ranch. With what's at stake, I feel sure your *backers* who're putting up the money wouldn't want to risk everything upon a bunch hired just because they supported the Union, rather than former Johnny Rebs who know practically everything that will be needed to be known if the buffalo are to be collected and delivered."

"He has a point," claimed "Ivan Boski," the tallest, bulki-est, and most prominently aquiline-featured of the quartet. His manner was closer to conferring a favor upon a hired hand by agreeing, rather than speaking about an important member of their party. "And, anyway, Kevin, with what's in store for them when we've got the herd close enough to where we want it, I'd think you would prefer them being peckerwoods."

"That's true," Morrell supported. "And having it done by some of that Rebel scum makes the end result so much more satisfying."

If he had not already long since arrived at the conclusion, looking at his associates and listening to the conversation Johnson would have deduced why he was being paid a good sum of money to accompany them. The men financing the scheme had realized that not one of the six possessed the ability to handle negotiations and deal with the kind of specialists needed to give the project a good chance of succeeding.

Born into wealthy families of Boston and Newark, New Jersey, respectively, Roddy and Morrell had discovered they lacked the intelligence and force of personality to succeed in the business world. Therefore, they had developed into radical activists of the worst kind. Professing a desire to improve the lot of the underprivileged working-class masses, they were arrant snobs who patronized and looked down upon the very people they were supposed to be helping.

Imbued with a hatred for everybody who did not adhere blindly to their point of view, the Easterners included the majority of Southerners in this category. As far as they were concerned, anybody who served—or was even remotely connected—with the former Confederate States was beyond the pale. In this, they included the men who possessed the requisite knowledge to move the buffalo. Therefore, neither of them could be counted upon to obtain the services of a trail drive crew composed of Texans.

Far from being recently arrived immigrants from Bohemia, a subterfuge insisted upon by the New Englander, the other four had been born in different parts of the United States. Furthermore, the likeness between their features and those of Indians on various illustrations seen by the desk clerk was far from being a coincidence. "Romanov" had first seen the light of day on the Yakima reservation in southern Washington State. Born in the Indian nations of Oklahoma, "Budapest" and "Boski" were respectively of Osage and Creek parentage. Coming in height and physique between the Yakima and the Creek, but with features more Mongoloid in aspect than either, "Petrovich" was of Onondaga Iroquoian birth.

The fathers of each Indian were wealthy members of their tribes who had accepted that the continued rule by the United States government was unavoidable and elected to prepare their offspring to make the most of such a state of affairs. With that objective in mind, their sons had been sent to various cities in the East to be educated. While the College for Indians in which they eventually enrolled and met produced many graduates willing to work toward bringing accord between their respective nations and the "paleface" population who would be their neighbors, none of the four could be included in that number.

Having failed in competitive society, like Roddy and Morrell, the quartet had decided the only hope of gaining the power they craved was by other means. Therefore, they had found the company of white radical-intellectuals very much to their taste. Such people were only too willing to listen to and spread the stories they told of how their respective tribes had been persecuted, while just as eagerly accepting denials of any happenings that might serve to discredit the image they painted of themselves as poor and downtrodden "noble Redmen." By adopting and playing to the hilt such double standards, they had become prominent among the political activists—although the term had not yet come into usage—who were bringing the College into disrepute. None of the four had devised the scheme that depended upon the transference of a herd of buffalo to a new location, but all were soon actively involved in its implementation.

This, in its turn, had brought the four young Indians into contact with Johnson!

Far from being a radical-intellectual, the New Englander was a competent and successful confidence trickster. He had been hired by the organizers of the scheme because, unlike any of them, he had spent sufficient time west of the Mississippi River to know where to look for and how best to deal with the kind of men who would be required to move the buffalo a considerable distance.

Johnson had not been enamored of being accompanied by any of the young radicals, particularly the Indians. Even before setting out, despite supposedly working for a common cause, they had constantly been at one another's throats over matters of tribal pride. Therefore, he had made it a condition of his acceptance that—as he had pointed out to Morrell and Roddy at the Fair Lady Saloon—he was given command of the party. Having been disinclined to take the risks of going themselves, the men who were financing the scheme had acceded to his terms.

While in the East, the quartet always dressed in the full regalia of their respective tribes with the intention of—as a later generation would put it—establishing their ethnic origins. Wise in the ways of the West, the New Englander had insisted they did not attempt to do so while there. He had pointed out that having four Indians from widely separated nations traveling together would attract unwanted attention and could lead to trouble with local populations. To avoid either possibility, he had made them have their hair cut to conform with white fashion and wear garments that would allow them to pass without arousing undue notice. Knowing their physical appearances would still require explanation, he had concocted the story of their having come from Bohemia and given them names that might have originated in that country.

"It will be *satisfying,* I'll admit," Roddy conceded, breaking into Johnson's train of thought. However, contemplating the fate awaiting the men hired to drive the herd, another point occurred to him. "But what about those other two peckerwood bastards who were brought into it?"

"Hell, yes!" Morrell exclaimed. "Once they start telling people about us having the bison moved, somebody is sure to guess the rest of it when news of the prophecy begins to get out."

"Captain Fog gave his word that they wouldn't talk about it," the New Englander pointed out.

"And, of course," Morrell sneered, "*you* believe he'll keep it!"

"I do," Johnson replied definitely, satisfied the scheme would be too far advanced to be stopped by the time Dusty Fog realized what was happening.

"Well, I *don't!*" Roddy declared and, after the other young Easterner had muttered concurrence, went on, "Nor am I willing to jeopardize what we're doing by giving them a chance to expose us."

"And what do *you* intend to do about it?" the New Englander challenged.

"They can't talk if they're *dead!*" the fair-haired Easterner said cryptically.

"So *you* aim to kill them?" Johnson suggested, his tone derisive.

"Not *personally,*" Roddy admitted. "But finding somebody who'll be willing to do it for money will be easy in a town like this."

"Why not go and look for a feller from a circus who'll have his pet elephant stamp them to death?" the New Englander growled. "Because you've as much chance of doing it as you have of finding anybody out there who'll be willing to even think of going after Dusty Fog and the Ysabel Kid the way you want."

4

SOMEBODY'S *SHOT* LON!

"I tell you, Doc," said the blond youngster whose only known name was Waco, interrupting the story being told by the Ysabel Kid while strolling along the adequately illuminated sidewalk toward the brightly lit front of the Fair Lady Saloon. They were accompanied by the exceptionally handsome blond giant Mark Counter and a friend belonging to the Wedge trail crew. Having been attending to the well-being of their horses, they were on their way to join Freddie Woods and Dusty Fog for supper and an evening's entertainment. "When those greasers around the cockpit got a look at that runty 'n' scrawny lil ole barnyard rooster's Lon dumped out of his sack, you was like' to've heard 'em laughing all the way to the Kansas line, did the wind be blowing right. Which they laughed even louder when one of 'em put in what he claimed to be the champion fighting cock of the whole world, *including* Texas."

"Well now, boy, I can't gainsay's they was laughing more

than a mite," conceded the Indian-dark and black-clad Texan, with the air of one who considered an injustice was being done and must be put to rights. "But *you* can't gainsay neither's how good ole Tornado didn't right soon show 'em what he was made of."

"Was I a gambling man, which nobody's ever known me to be," Marvin Eldridge "Doc" Leroy claimed, his voice redolent of suspicion as he looked from the Kid to Waco and back, "I'd just bet you're going to tell me's how your bird whipped every God damned feather off the champion."

About the same height and build as the Kid, with an equal suggestion of being far from puny, the clothing worn by the speaker was also that of a working cowhand from Texas. Except when a situation required such an attitude, his good-looking features implied a much more studious and serious nature than was the case. Although they were pallid, this was due to his skin having a resistance to becoming tanned rather than through leading a sedentary life that kept him indoors most of the time. His hair was black, as was his neatly trimmed mustache. To allow unimpeded access to the ivory butt of the Colt Civilian Model Peacemaker revolver in the fast-draw holster of his well-designed gun belt, the right side of the loose-fitting jacket he had on was stitched back. In his left hand was the kind of small black leather bag in which medical practitioners carried their instruments and other items needed in their professional capacity when away from the office.

Having spent considerably longer than he had intended discussing a newly developed medical technique with the well-informed local doctor after assisting in a difficult delivery of a baby, the Wedge trail hand had gone to a livery stable where many of the visiting Texans left their horses. On his arrival, he discovered that the other members of his crew had already finished their chores and departed. Therefore, since his medical activities of the afternoon had caused him to miss seeing them at the Fair Lady Saloon, he had been delighted to find the three members of the OD Connected ranch's already almost legendary floating outfit on the premises. Not only were Mark and the Kid friends of long standing, having served as peace officers with him early in their acquaintance, but learning they had many interests in common, he had come to enjoy Waco's company just as much.

With their respective tasks completed, impelled by the loyalty and pride that the majority of Texas' cowhands felt toward their employers, Doc had announced that the Wedge crew had already been hired to handle another trail drive. Asked by the blond youngster who "on God's good earth would be danged fool enough to take on such a no-account bunch," he had countered by pointing out he said it was the Wedge and not the OD Connected selected for the chore. When Mark had inquired where they would be going, knowing the question did not spring from a desire to obtain information that might be used in an attempt to cut them out, Doc had had to admit Stone Hart had neither disclosed their destination nor even who had hired them.

Despite having guessed there was a connection between the hiring of the Wedge and the conversation with the three Easterners in which he and Dusty had been called to participate on entering the Fair Lady Saloon, the Kid had kept the thought to himself. From the looks they had directed his way, he surmised that the blond giant and Waco suspected the two events were related in some way. However, as the small Texan had explained why he and the Kid were not at liberty to divulge what had taken place when asked to join the trail boss, neither had attempted to satisfy his curiosity by asking further questions.

Leaving the livery stable and making a leisurely way through the busy main business section of the town toward the Fair Lady Saloon, the four friends had talked about some of the things they had done since last being in each other's company. When the Kid had started to describe how he had become involved in a cockfight held at a small town near the Rio Grande, Waco could not resist the temptation to intervene.

With their destination coming into view on the opposite side of the street, the Wedge trail hand had injected his comment. Knowing the black-dressed Texan, he was convinced the explanation would be far from ordinary and well worth hearing.

"Well, no," the Kid confessed, after a dramatic momentary pause. His manner implied a somewhat defensive defiance as he continued, "Being raised allus to speak up truthful' true, I don't reckon's how I can rightly come straight on out and say's ole Tornado *won*."

"He for certain sure *didn't* win," Waco confirmed.

"Maybe he didn't, but he didn't *lose* neither," the Indian-dark Texan countered and, although he refrained from adding the words "so there" audibly, they were suggested by his manner.

"I don't want to sound all nosy like," Doc asserted, genuinely interested in getting to the bottom of the mystery. "But, seeing's how he didn't *win* and he didn't *lose* neither, would I be wrong in saying they must've gone to a draw and standoff?"

"Well, no, not *exactly*," the blond youngster answered. "Comes down to being pushed to a real sharp point, I wouldn't want to go so far's to say it went to a draw 'n' standoff neither."

"I'll be switched if this hasn't got me kissed off against the cushion!" the Wedge hand declared, swinging a gaze filled with puzzlement from Waco to the Kid and back before turning to Mark for enlightenment. "If that bird's I'm start-

ing to wish I'd *never* heard about didn't win, lose, or draw,
what the Sam Hill did he do?"

"Don't look at *me!*" the blond giant requested, his deep
voice having the timbre indicative of a good education. "I
know this pair a whole heap too well to've gotten mixed up
in their fool doings, so I stayed well clear of them."

"There's some, 'specially me, who'd say you showed real
good sense!" Doc claimed and once more studied the black-
clad Texan and youngster. "I just *know* I'm going to hate
myself for asking, but maybe one of you pair would like to
tell me about it?"

"Why I'd count it a honor 'n' privilege to do just that," the
Kid obliged. "Ole Tornado's one mighty smart bird, as birds
go. So, he took one look at them sharp 'n' long steel spikes's
was fastened to the champion fighting cock's legs and he lit a
shuck out of there like the devil chased by holy water."

"You mean he just up and *ran away*?" Doc asked, although certain there was much more to the story than that.

"He did *not* just 'up and run away'!" the Kid denied indignantly.

"It surely sounds to me that he didn't do nothing else but
up and run away," the Wedge hand insisted. "But, knowing
you, I don't reckon it'll be any place in a long country mile of
that simple."

"It for surely *wasn't* that simple," the Indian-dark Texan
claimed. "Like I said, ole Tornado's a right smart bird, as
birds go. So, same's I told all them greasers when they
started reckoning's how he'd turned tail 'n' run, soon's he
saw he was being put up against a world-champion fighting
cock's'd been given the edge by toting a couple of knives, he
concluded to head for home and fetch some for hisself."

"Like you said!" Doc growled, his voice redolent of dis-
gust, although he was needing all his considerable skill as a
poker player to prevent the amusement he was feeling from

showing. "Ole Tornado's a right smart bird, as birds go. So, the further he goes and sooner, the better place the world'll be—and he should take you pair of knob-heads with him."

"That wasn't *nice!*" Waco claimed in an aggrieved tone. "But, was we to tell him's he's uncouth, I'm willing to bet he'd say he's just as couth as we are, or maybe even couther."

"Whcc dogie!" the Wedge trail hand exclaimed, staring with what might have been admiration at the younger blonde. "Where did *you* learn five-dollar-a-throw words like 'uncouth,' 'couth,' and 'couther'?"

"Miz Freddie told me's I was uncouth one time," Waco replied. "And, way she looked at me when she said it, being *real* fast 'bout things like that, comes four, five days'd gone by, I got around to figuring *maybe* it wasn't what some folks's call ni—"

The flow of levity was brought to an abrupt close!

A rifle cracked from the mouth of an alley separating the Fair Lady Saloon from its neighbor on the left!

Muzzle flash glowed red, pointing in the direction of the five Texans!

As the Kid was about to step from the sidewalk to cross the street, his head was jerked sideways and the black hat was torn from it by a bullet!

*   *   *

Even though this was long before an age when a certain very vocal political philosophy would seek to elevate human sexuality to being the most praiseworthy of human attributes, the attractive little blonde entering the elegant sitting room on the second floor of the Fair Lady Saloon found nothing surprising or even to be objected to in the sight of Mulrooney's mayor and most respected citizen being engaged in a passionate embrace with the *segundo* and trail boss of one of the largest ranches in Texas.

Having come from England with "Freddie Woods"—the alias selected by the Right Honorable Winifred Amelia Besgrove-Woodstole when electing to make her new home in the United States of America—Barbara "Babsy" Smith knew and fully approved of her close relationship with Dusty Fog.

The sale of the OD Connected ranch's herd had been concluded without difficulty, in spite of the Wedge having reached Mulrooney first, before the visit paid by the small Texan and his three *amigos* to the Fair Lady Saloon that afternoon. Nevertheless, there had been other matters demanding Dusty's attention. In addition to having paid off the cowhands who had been his trail crew, he had had to make courtesy calls upon Town Marshal Kail Beauregard—who had succeeded him in that official capacity—and various other civic dignitaries with whom he had become acquainted and was on good terms with during the hectic days when he and his companions of Ole Devil Hardin's floating outfit were responsible for enforcing the law in the town. With so many urgent matters demanding his attention he had, for once, accepted an offer from Waco to attend to the big paint stallion that was his favorite horse instead of attending to him personally. Under normal circumstances, he would not have allowed any other person to take care of an animal he had selected to be his working mount.

With his various affairs brought to a satisfactory conclusion shortly after sundown, the small Texan had been at liberty to turn his attention to personal matters!

On his return to the saloon, Dusty was carrying his low-horned and double-girthed Texas-style saddle. Despite the apparent ease with which he was handling it, even discounting those items of his property attached to it, this was a considerable weight. A thirty-foot-long rope, of three-strand Manila fiber laid extra hard for strength and smoothness, was coiled and strapped to the horn. In the boot at the left side of the skirts, butt pointing to the rear for a rapid removal when dismounting, was a Winchester Model of 1873 carbine. Fastened to the cantle was his bedroll and war bag wrapped in a sheet of waterproof tarpaulin.

Despite custom having greatly increased while he was away, Freddie had accompanied the small Texan to her private accommodation on the second floor. While crossing to the stairs, he had looked without success for Stone Hart. Although the trail boss of the Wedge had not been on the premises, the three Easterners with whom they had talked were seated at a table by the left-side front window. However, apart from Walter Johnson having nodded a greeting upon seeing him glancing in their direction, they had given no indication of being aware of his presence. This had not worried him. Having developed a dislike for Kevin Roddy and Francis Morrell, he had felt disinclined to attempt to renew their brief acquaintance and considered the sentiment to be mutual.

Entering the suite reserved for the owner's personal use, the small Texan had placed his property in the wardrobe of the bedroom. Freddie and he had become very close during the early days of Mulrooney's existence as a trail-end town and the relationship had grown warmer with each subsequent visit. Therefore, he was now accorded a privilege of being accommodated in her living quarters.

After having participated in the British tradition of "tea," albeit at a slightly later hour than usual, Dusty and the beautiful black-haired Englishwoman remained in the sitting room instead of going downstairs. They had talked of their various activities since last meeting. Then the conversation had turned to the future. Without having reached any decisions upon the subject uppermost in both their thoughts, they had become more romantically inclined.

The arrival of Babsy Smith had interrupted the interlude!

"Yes, Babsy," Freddie greeted, extracting herself from the arms of the small Texan without any hurry or evidence of wishing to avoid being seen in such a fashion. "Is anything wrong?"

"Not a thing, Miss Freddie," replied the curvaceous, close to buxom and vivacious young woman, her accent being that of one who had by tradition been born within hearing distance of Bow Bells in London. She wore the attire of a saloongirl. However, despite being a talented singer and entertainer, she was content to serve in the capacity of lady's maid for the black-haired beauty. "Only Cookie wants to know when the boys'll be getting here. She says supper'll soon be ready and, knowing her, she'll be proper narked if it gets spoiled because they're late."

"I'll go take a look out the window to find out if they're coming yet," Dusty offered. "I don't have any notion what that 'proper narked' might be, 'cepting I've a sneaking notion it doesn't mean Cookie'll be all pleasured up should her meal get spoiled. So, if they're not in sight, I'll drift on over to the livery stable and chase them along on the run."

Starting to cross the luxuriously and tastefully fitted sitting room, hand in hand with Freddie, the small Texan glanced at the glass-fronted cabinet on the right side of the French windows. To anybody less familiar with her, it might have appeared an unusual item of furniture for her to own. It held a brace of magnificent Purdey shotguns, a heavy-caliber British-made Holland & Holland double-barreled rifle, three Winchesters, two ivory-handled Colt Civilian Model Peacemakers, and boxes of ammunition for them. He knew that, although the Winchesters were not kept loaded—as to have done so continuously would have ruined the magazine springs—the shotguns, rifle, and revolvers were in case of an emergency. He was also aware that she could use each type of firearm with considerable accuracy should the need arise.

Liberating his hand from the gentle grasp of the English-woman, Dusty drew apart the drapes that covered the glass-paneled windows. Despite there being a veranda with a wooden guardrail outside, the opposite sidewalk and buildings were in view. Sufficient light was coming from those business premises that were open for them to be able to see that the men they were looking for were approaching.

"Just look at them," Freddie remarked. "Sauntering along as if they had all the time in the world."

"Why sure," the small Texan agreed, identifying the fourth member of the party. "What'll you bet that they don't blame Doc for delaying them, if we tell them they're late?"

"Why don't you ask me to bet night doesn't follow day?" Freddie replied with a smile. "I'll say one thing about you, darling, you really want an edge when you offer a bet. Although I will admit that Waco in particular can be a bit more original than that when there's an excuse to be made."

"That he can," Dusty agreed, but there was neither sting nor animosity to the words. Like all the other members of the floating outfit, he regarded the blond youngster as a favorite younger brother. "But he claims he wasn't nearly so ready a liar before he met up with us."

"I can well imagine that," the Englishwoman declared, watching the quartet turning to leave the sidewalk and cross the street. Then, seeing the Ysabel Kid reel and lose his hat, even though she was unable to hear the crack of the rifle from the left side alley, she guessed what had happened and gasped, "My God, somebody's *shot* Lon!"

Having reached the same conclusion, the small Texan did not reply. Instead, cursing himself for having left his gun belt in the bedroom with his other property, he reached down to

twist the key in the lock of the French windows. Telling
Freddie to get the "elephant gun" from the cabinet for him,
he lunged through. As he arrived on the veranda, a bullet
was fired from behind the signboard on the roof of the building at the other side of the street.

5

THEY'VE GOT DUSTY
AS WELL

Despite being taken completely unaware by the shot, Mark Counter, Waco, and Doc Leroy were not frozen into immobility by panic!

Having spent much of their lives in precarious situations, the three Texans reacted rapidly and in accordance with the way they respectively believed the situation should be handled!

The Ysabel Kid was sent staggering by the bullet to collide with the blond giant, but Mark hardly so much as swayed under the unexpected impact. Instead, scooping the crumpling body of his black-dressed *amigo* into his arms with no more apparent effort than if lifting a newborn baby, he swung and raced for the shelter offered by the corner of the building they had been passing. While doing so, such was the intense loyalty the members of Ole Devil Hardin's floating outfit felt for one another, he twisted his massive torso to act as a shield in case the unknown assailant meant to continue firing in their direction.

Throwing a quick glance, Waco discovered that the Kid had been hit. Although he now only rarely employed the profanity that had accompanied practically every sentence before he had joined the elite core of the OD Connected ranch's crew, an obscenity burst from the youngster. However, he did not restrict himself merely to cursing. Even as he was speaking, sending both hands to sweep the staghorn-butted Colt Artillery Model Peacemaker revolvers from their contoured holsters, he sprang from the sidewalk. Armed and ready to open fire by the time he alighted, he set off across the street. Running swiftly at an angle over the wheel-rutted surface, he was making for the alley from which the shot had come.

With the ivory-handled Colt Civilian Model Peacemaker seeming to join his right fist in midair, so rapidly did he bring it from its holster, the Wedge trail hand was on the point of accompanying the departing blond youngster. His medical training had not yet been completed, but the instincts he had already acquired caused him to change his mind before he could put the first inclination into being. Knowing the Kid had shown signs of being struck in the head by the bullet, the gravity of the situation was all too obvious to him. He was aware that, should the wound not be fatal, seconds delayed in starting to attend to it could spell the difference between life and death. Therefore, he turned and dashed after Mark instead of going with Waco.

Making for the opening, seeing the barrel of a Winchester rifle being withdrawn beyond the end of the Fair Lady Saloon, the blond youngster's attention was diverted to the flood of light that appeared through a window on the second floor as the drapes were drawn open. From his recollection of the building's layout, he concluded it was originating from the sitting room of Freddie Woods's private living accommodation.

Almost as if wishing to verify the assumption for Waco, having jerked open the French windows, Dusty Fog came into view on the veranda!

Before the blond youngster could call out to the small Texan, coming from behind him this time, he heard another rifle shot!

Once again, Waco discovered that he was not the intended target!

Before the youngster could feel any relief over not having been selected by the second would-be assailant, who—he deduced from the sound—was situated well above ground level, alarm flooded through him as he saw another member of the floating outfit was pitching sideways!

"Oh my God!" Waco breathed, his voice filled with torment. "They've got Dusty as well!"

* * *

"So much for that white bastard, Johnson!" Hugo Budapest announced, twisting himself and his smoking Winchester Model of 1873 rifle behind the right edge of the signboard after having seen Dusty Fog plunging out of the light from the open French windows on being fired at by him. "Getting the beef-head son of a bitch was easy!"

"The hell you got him!" contradicted Ivan Boski, keeping watch from the other end of the convenient hiding place on the roof overlooking the frontage of the Fair Lady Saloon. "You missed the bastard and he's only dived into the shadows. Pass me the rifle and I'll soon show you how to finish him off."

"I will *not*, you could've bought one for yourself and didn't!" the Osage refused, only approving of the "share and share alike" philosophy preached by his kind when it would be himself on the receiving end. "I'll give him another, if it'll make *you* feel any easier. But I *know* I've already nailed him."

"Then do it, instead of just talking!" the Creek commanded savagely. "Somebody below will have heard you shoot—"

"You get scared awful easy!" Budapest sneered, but being equally aware of the possibility he decided against a delay that was merely intended to show his disinclination to take orders from a member of what he considered a lesser tribe to his own.

The brief, yet acrimonious, conversation was typical of the attitude all four Indians displayed toward one another. Although supposedly united in a common cause, age-old tribal rivalries and their own selfish, self-important natures made each determined to exhibit what he considered to be his superiority over the others. It was a realization of the danger posed to the scheme by their mutually argumentative behavior that had led the men financing them to insist upon Walter Johnson being in command of the party.

Earlier that afternoon, faced by the pessimistic assessment of their chances by the New Englander, the younger conspirators had grudgingly conceded he possessed a far greater local knowledge than any of them. Therefore, they had reluctantly given up the idea of hiring men to remove what they still insisted was a threat to the scheme, especially as they had no idea of how to hire local gunmen. Instead, goaded by an ill-advised remark from Johnson, who had made it obvious he doubted whether any of them possessed the necessary ability or courage to deal with the causes of their concern, they had declared they would do it themselves. Although he had stated his disapproval and repeated his assertion that there was no reason for any such attempt, he had discovered they were adamant and would go ahead without his assistance if necessary. Therefore, he had con-

cluded that self-preservation dictated he should not leave
the planning of the venture in their hands.

Everything the New Englander knew about such matters
warned him of the very grave danger that was likely to be
encountered when up against men with the considerable experience of gunfighting possessed by Dusty Fog and the
Ysabel Kid. Even discounting the practically unavoidable
participation by their almost as competent companions, either would prove an exceptionally capable and dangerous
adversary. Nothing Johnson had seen of his associates led
him to assume that, collectively or individually, they were
even close to being a match for such high-class and effective
competition.

Having had such a consideration in mind, while willing to
have devoted the majority of his wiles toward helping the
young men to achieve their purpose, Johnson had also decided it was mandatory to direct a proportion of his attention to lessen the chance of being implicated personally in
case of failure. With the latter point in mind, he had been
grateful for the precautions already taken to prevent his
connection with the Indians from becoming known. At his
instigation, he, Kevin Roddy, and Francis Morrell had arrived at Mulrooney the day before the "Bohemians." When
paying the visit to the Grimsdyke Temperance Hotel, he had
contrived to reach their rooms without being seen by the
desk clerk or anybody else on the premises and had intended
to ensure his departure was just as unobserved.

There had been suspicious looks from the four Indians
when informed by the New Englander that he and the other
two white men would not be playing an active part in the
proposed assassination. He had pointed out that, if any of
them were to do so and should be seen and identified, it
would prove detrimental to the remainder of the scheme.
Playing upon their pretense of being fully trained warriors,

despite knowing none of them had acquired the requisite skills to justify the claim, he had persuaded the quartet that they possessed a knowledge of fighting that he and the two younger Easterners lacked.

Getting his way on the vital issue of active participation, Johnson had stated that the quartet would carry out their assignments dressed as cowhands. All the necessary attire and firearms could be purchased without difficulty in the town and the disguise would prevent the real motive being suspected when the local peace officers, who he had warned were led by a man far from being a stupid country bumpkin, questioned witnesses. To further ensure their acquiescence and cooperation, he had promised that he would pay for everything they required out of the funds put at his disposal by their backers to cover the incidental expenses of the trip.

To give Johnson his due, even though motivated by the proviso he had set for his own welfare, he had done everything he could to give the Indians the best possible chance of achieving their purpose!

Having arranged to meet the four "Bohemians" elsewhere later to explain how the assassination was to be carried out, the Easterners had been successful in leaving the hotel without being seen by any of its other occupants. On returning to the Fair Lady Saloon, he had discovered that the Texans with whom he had spoken earlier had left to attend to their respective affairs. Then, without any of the donors realizing they were being pumped for it, he had continued to put to use all his considerable experience to set about acquiring the rest of the information he required. From what he had learned about the present locations and most probable future activities of the intended victims, backed by a careful study of the surrounding terrain, he had been able to concoct a plan that he had considered would fulfill their needs.

Leaving Roddy and Morrell at the saloon to watch out for

the two Texans, Johnson had attended the rendezvous with the Indians. Although he had given them sufficient money to purchase the necessary clothing, plus a handgun and Winchester Model of 1873 rifle apiece, he had found that only Budapest and Peter Romanov had obtained the shoulder arm. Having done as the New Englander instructed, by going to different stores to fill their respective needs, Boski and Rudolph Petrovich claimed the prices were so high at the establishments that received their custom that they could only afford a secondhand Colt Cavalry Model Peacemaker each after having purchased their cowhand-style attire. Refraining from stating his belief that they were lying and had pocketed the difference, Johnson saw that they had all taken one piece of advice he had given. Knowing that wearing the specialized footwear of a cowhand required considerable use to ensure ease of movement, he had warned against buying high-heeled, sharp-toed boots, and none had done so. Grateful that they had obeyed him up to a point, he had told them where to go and how to achieve their purpose.

Basing his plans upon what he had learned and seen, Johnson had known from which direction the Ysabel Kid was almost certain to return from the livery barn. Making a shrewd guess that he would not cross the street earlier, the New Englander had instructed Petrovich and Romanov to lie in wait down an alley near the Fair Lady Saloon. He did not know that, wanting to make their task as easy as possible, they had selected a position much closer than he had intended.

Budapest and Boski, on the other hand, had done exactly as they were told!

Having learned that Dusty Fog would be in Freddie Woods's private living accommodation at the front of the saloon, the New Englander had taken advantage of the second floor of the building opposite being unoccupied after sundown. An investigation had informed him that access to the flat roof was rendered less difficult by an outside flight of stairs leading to one of the offices at the rear. Following orders, the Osage and the Creek had attained their hiding place from which they had kept watch until their selected victim appeared on the veranda to investigate the shooting of his companion.

From what they had heard on the street below their position, and from the sight of the small Texan coming through the French windows, the two young Indians concluded that Johnson had been correct in his assumptions. However, they were in less accord over the result of the shot fired by Budapest.

Easing himself and the Winchester cautiously from behind the edge of the signboard, the Osage gave a hiss of satisfaction when unable to locate Dusty Fog. Then he became aware that the owner of the saloon had come onto the veranda. What was more, she was already lining a weapon in his direction. Noticing it had double barrels, he decided there was no cause for concern. At the distance that was separating them, he felt convinced the cloud of shot she discharged would have spread to such an extent that he was unlikely to be hit. Or, even if any of the tiny balls should do so, they would be almost at the end of their flight and traveling too slowly to do any harm.

Satisfied that he had nothing to fear from the beautiful and elegantly clad woman, Budapest returned his attention to searching for what he had no doubt would prove to be the lifeless body of the small Texan.

*   *   *

Ivan Boski had drawn a more accurate conclusion than either his companion or Waco with regard to the shot fired by Budapest.

Hearing the eerie "splat!" caused by what he knew to be a

bullet splitting the air close to his head, Dusty Fog responded to the emergency with an alacrity equaling that shown by his companions a few seconds earlier!

Being without weapons of any kind, until Freddie Woods could carry out his request by delivering the British-made Holland & Holland double-barreled rifle from the cabinet in the sitting room, the small Texan threw himself toward the bench seat on the right side of the French windows. Although it did not offer either shelter or protection from the man on the opposite roof, he was more concerned with getting out of the light coming from behind him and into the shadows alongside the wall.

Still inside the building, the beautiful black-haired woman was also made aware of the danger. The bullet that had so narrowly missed Dusty passed between her and Babsy Smith as the little Cockney started to dash forward. Instead of letting out screeches and descending into a state of terrified immobility—practically the only responses to gunfire allowed a heroine in the majority of action-escapism-adventure fiction—each continued to follow the course to which she had committed herself.

Jerking open the doors of the glass-fronted cabinet, Freddie snatched out the weapon requested by Dusty. Drawing back its hammers with deft skill, while striding swiftly through the French windows, she called for the little blonde to fetch the Purdey shotguns in case they too should be required. Furthermore, in keeping with her birth and upbringing as a member of one of Britain's oldest noble families, she did not restrict her activities to merely handing over the firearm and withdrawing to safety. Realizing she might not be presented with an opportunity to do so, she was ready, willing, and capable of taking action herself.

Like the small Texan and the blond youngster on the street below, the Englishwoman had assessed the general

direction from which the shot had come. Almost as soon as
she emerged from the sitting room, aided by her summation,
she set about the task of locating the would-be killer. Deciding the signboard on the roof of the building at the other
side of the street was the most likely possibility, she turned
her gaze immediately in that direction. For a moment, she
thought that she was wrong. Then a movement drew her
attention to its right side. Watching the straight line of the
edge start to develop a slight bulge, she realized how this
was caused. The man had withdrawn behind the signboard
for some reason after shooting at Dusty, but was looking
around it once more.

The discovery convinced Freddie that there would not be
sufficient time for her to pass the Holland & Holland to the
small Texan!

The sound of the weapon across the street had been characteristic of a Winchester, not one of the various single-shot
rifles of larger caliber!

Therefore, the would-be killer was practically certain to
have several more bullets ready for immediate disposal!

What was more, anybody on the veranda was in a most
exposed position from the opposite roof!

Swinging up the Holland & Holland, with the smooth
speed indicative of considerable practice, the beautiful Englishwoman was completely oblivious of how incongruous
her behavior—taken in conjunction with the elegant and
revealingly form-fitting gown she had donned for the evening's entertainment downstairs—might have struck a
chance onlooker. She had no thoughts for anything other
than what she was doing. By the time she had settled the
brass butt plate against her thinly covered right shoulder,
while her right thumb was instinctively operating the manual
safety catch positioned conveniently on the top tang of the

stock, she was already gazing along the rib between the twin barrels.

A moment after her employer had located the would-be killer, Babsy came through the French windows. Showing a surprising grasp of the situation, she had amended the order she was given. While she was carrying one of the Purdey shotguns in her right hand, the left was grasping the ivory handle of a Colt Civilian Model Peacemaker. Turning her worried gaze to where she had seen Dusty disappearing in a plunging dive, she gave a gasp of relief on discovering her fears for his well-being were unfounded. However, instead of delaying until she had expressed her feelings verbally, she swerved in his direction holding forward the weapons.

Paying not the slightest attention to what her maid was doing, although she would have approved of the alteration to her instructions, Freddie was prepared to make the most of the firearm she was holding regardless of its shortcomings for the task she had set herself.

By the standards of the day, despite its caliber being .465, the Holland & Holland held by the Englishwoman was considered too light to qualify for the title "elephant gun" employed by the small Texan when he had asked for it to be given to him. Nevertheless, it had been intended for a similar purpose to firearms in that category. It was meant not only to kill, but also to knock down almost instantaneously a fairly large and dangerous animal at close quarters. Therefore, while one of the finest examples of that particular type of rifle made anywhere in the world, it was equipped with only the most basic open "sporting" sights and these were not conducive to accuracy over long distances. Nor, to be fair to the manufacturers, were they designed to be.

Closing her left eye, conscious of the very pressing need to get off a shot as quickly as possible, Freddie concentrated upon aligning the notch of the simple rear sight with the small knob set on the center of the rib near the muzzle!

In spite of the competence she was displaying in handling the rifle, the Englishwoman was all too aware that dealing with the situation was far from being a sure thing!

6

THAT'S A *MISTAKE*

Even as the fresh flood of alarm was assailing Waco, he realized that Dusty Fog was merely diving for cover and not going down as a result of having been hit by the bullet from the roof of the building across the street!

Support for the supposition was provided by Freddie Woods as she emerged onto the veranda of the Fair Lady Saloon. To the blond youngster's way of thinking, her behavior was significant. He found nothing in the least surprising about her carrying one of the double-barreled firearms, which he guessed correctly would be the Holland & Holland .465 rifle, from the cabinet near the French windows of the sitting room. However, competent and quick thinking as he knew her to be under normal circumstances, he felt sure she could not have retained her usual composure if the small Texan—with whom he knew her to be on terms of considerable intimacy—was dead, or even injured.

Further evidence was supplied by the sight of Babsy Smith

when, carrying one of the Purdey shotguns and a Colt Peace-maker, she followed her employer into view. Knowing her as well as he had very good cause to, Waco was equally con-vinced she would have displayed distress if the glance she took had established that Dusty was injured or worse.

Satisfied and greatly relieved by the discovery that the man he admired more than anybody else in the world was all right, the youngster continued to run toward the corner of the saloon from behind which the Ysabel Kid had been shot. Under the prevailing conditions, he considered he would be better employed in that direction and could leave dealing with the attacker on the roof to Freddie or Dusty. They were more suitably positioned on the veranda to do so than he was at street level.

On arriving at the entrance of the alley, ready to open fire with the Colt Artillery Model Peacemakers he was carrying, Waco found the man who had shot the Kid was no longer in it. Despite various sounds from behind him, which implied he had drawn the correct solution over the most suitable way to have the second attacker dealt with, he could hear swiftly running footsteps going away to the right along the street to the rear of the buildings.

Not just one set, the youngster estimated, but two!

Discovering he would be up against more than a single man did not deter Waco!

While not wildly reckless, the youngster was aware of his own capabilities if it should come to gunplay. In any event, he was determined to get at least a close enough view of the fleeing pair to have a chance of identifying them later should they succeed in evading his pursuit.

Arriving on the street at the back of the saloon, Waco saw two figures entering an alley a short distance away at the other side. They wore Stetsons and attire similar to his own. However, clearly their footwear was lacking the functional high heels that caused a cowhand to have a distinctive gait unmistakable to anybody as familiar as he was with other members of that hard-working, hard-riding, and hard-playing fraternity. Even discounting the suggestions that the pair were obviously in full flight, they were the pair he was seeking. That was apparent from the Winchester Model of 1873 rifle—identifiable even at a distance by having a steel frame, instead of the brass that had given its predecessor, the Model of 1866, the sobriquet "Old Yellowboy"—carried by the taller. Furthermore, the other was grasping a Colt Cavalry Model Peacemaker revolver in his right hand, which under the prevailing circumstances was hardly an indication that he was merely hurrying somewhere for an innocent purpose.

Following the men as swiftly as his legs would carry him, Waco wished he were astride his big paint stallion instead of being afoot!

The sentiment did not arise from the natural preference of every cowhand to ride rather than walk!

Being seated on the horse, the youngster realized, would have allowed him to overtake the two men with greater ease. Or, aided by his remembrance of the town's geography— acquired while he was serving as a deputy marshal under Dusty Fog—he might be granted an opportunity to go around undetected and, instead of being compelled to make his approach from behind as was sure to be expected, take them unawares somewhere ahead. To have been able to achieve this would have offered him a far better chance of capturing one, or maybe both, alive.

There had been a time, not too long gone by, when such a consideration would not have entered Waco's head!

However, that period had ended when the youngster was accepted as a member of Ole Devil Hardin's floating outfit!

Now, despite his deep concern for the well-being of the

Ysabel Kid, Waco could appreciate how useful it could prove to have at least one living captive able to tell why and at whose orders the ambush had been laid!

Accepting that he had no horse, the youngster kept moving. Once again, on arriving at the mouth of an alley along which his quarry had disappeared, he found they were no longer in view. Passing along, he located them hurrying into the gap between two more buildings. Realizing exactly where they were, he felt a sense of hope that was close to elation.

The chase had left the area of the town mainly given over to evening entertainment and was passing through business premises that had the appearance of already being closed for the night. Gazing around, Waco concluded that—unless his recollection was at fault, or alterations had been made since his last visit—provided they lacked his knowledge of the locality, the pair might make his task of catching up with them less difficult. Of course, if they should find themselves in the position he envisaged, dealing with them would be anything but a sure thing.

On reaching the appropriate corner and pausing to peer around, the youngster decided that the possibility had materialized!

Nobody was in sight in the gap between the buildings!

However, the sounds of footsteps had come to a halt and were being replaced by startled and angry exclamations!

"That's a *mistake,* you sons of bitches!" Waco breathed, resuming his advance. "You've got yourselves boxed in and've got to come out my way!"

The youngster knew what had caused the consternation!

The buildings between which the fleeing men had elected to pass and the pair to their immediate rear were the property of a large freight outfit. When Waco had last been in Mulrooney, although it was possible to go straight through and emerge in the lower-rent district, if one turned either right or left it would lead into what amounted to a *cul-de-sac*. Judging by what he had heard, he assumed this was still the case.

Probably wishing to avoid being exposed to gunfire by being silhouetted between the buildings, the two men had turned right into what they had believed to be another alley. Having done so, they had found the way was blocked by a high wooden fence without a gate.

Starting along the alley, the youngster watched the entrance from which the irate comments had come. He was ready to take whatever action might prove necessary when, as he believed was certain to happen, the two men returned his way. Then, probably attracted by the noise, somebody threw open the door that he had just passed in the left-side building. Flooding out, the light of a lamp projected his shadow across the gap he was approaching.

*   *   *

Allowing only the bare minimum period required to satisfy herself with her point of aim, Freddie Woods squeezed the forward set trigger. When purchasing the Holland & Holland .465 rifle, taking into account that her hand lacked the strength of the average masculine user, she had had the mechanism adjusted to a lower poundage of pressure than would usually have been the case. On tightening her forefinger, to the accompaniment of a much deeper roar than had been given by the Winchester across the street, the bullet in the right-side chamber was sent upon its way through the rifling grooves of the barrel.

Upon every other occasion when the black-haired and beautiful Englishwoman had fired the Holland & Holland, she had taken the precaution of wearing a jacket designed to offer protection against the powerful kick of the recoil. The wisdom of having had the garment made was brought home to her in no uncertain fashion. Nevertheless, despite giving a gasp of pain as the butt plate was thrust hard against her thinly covered shoulder, she concentrated upon bringing under control the rising twin barrels so as to be able to fire again if necessary.

Having selected the Colt Civilian Model Peacemaker, instead of the Purdey shotgun also offered to him by Babsy Smith, Dusty Fog grasped the butt in both hands and thumbed back the hammer. With the bellow of the Holland & Holland ringing in his ears, he lunged forward from the shadows to rest his wrists on top of the veranda's protective rail. Crouching with the revolver supported as an aid to sighting over the distance involved, he scanned the roof from which he had been fired upon.

Bringing down the barrels of the rifle, Freddie was not aware of what the small Texan was doing. All her attention was devoted to her own activities. Momentarily, the combination of the muzzle blast's red glow and swirling white gases from the detonated black powder was preventing her from seeing whether or not her shot had had any effect. She was all too aware that she would very soon learn the answer.

Regardless of having been used to carry out a type of shooting for which it was not designed, the Holland & Holland was proving adequate to deal with the situation. Instead of having tried to hit the small portion of the man that was exposed to her view across the street, the Englishwoman had aimed at the side of the signboard behind which she estimated the rest of his body must be. Although the limitations of the sights caused her to miss the point that would have produced the effect she was hoping to achieve, the result was not to be despised.

Striking the signboard at an angle, but just a trifle too high, the heavy bullet went through it as if it did not exist and passed just behind Hugo Budapest's head. However, such was the force of the impact, a cloud of splinters was flung from the wood. Several of them struck him in the side of the face. He frequently boasted of the stoicism shown by members of his race when sustaining injury, but his own reaction fell far short of justifying the claim. Letting out a shriek, he flung aside the Winchester rifle. Then, clutching at the affected area with both hands and shouting in his native tongue that he was blinded, he lurched from behind his place of concealment and toward the front edge of the roof.

Although unable to understand the Osage language employed by his companion, a sense of alarm assailed Ivan Boski. Under different circumstances, he would have derived much satisfaction from receiving proof that Budapest was wrong. Now, the discovery that Dusty Fog was unharmed, as he had claimed, was cause for concern rather than jubilation. The sight of the small Texan advancing to line a revolver over the veranda rail had warned him that, no matter what result had been achieved by Peter Romanov and Rudolph Petrovich, their own part of the assassination plot was a failure. What was more, he felt certain that retaliatory measures would very soon be commenced. Aware that their intended victims had numerous loyal friends in the town, including the local peace officers, according to Walter Johnson, he had no intention of trying to complete the task he and Budapest had been given. His every instinct declared that the roof was likely to become a death trap if he remained upon it.

On the point of taking a hurried departure, the young Creek darted a glance at his companion. He realized that his own freedom would be placed in jeopardy should he leave the Osage behind to be captured. However, having no idea of how serious an injury had been inflicted by the Englishwoman, he was equally disinclined to let himself be slowed down by Budapest. With the latter consideration uppermost in his thoughts, he cocked and raised the Colt Cavalry Peacemaker. Lining its seven-and-a-half-inch barrel to the best of his ability, he squeezed the trigger. The shot roared out and he saw Budapest, already teetering at the very edge of the roof, struck and knocked from it by the .45 bullet.

Making no attempt to go and ensure he had silenced the Osage permanently, Boski darted to the rear of the building. Tucking the revolver into the waistband of his blue jeans, he lowered himself to drop onto the flight of stairs by which they had gained access to the roof. While descending, he was alert for any indication that he had been seen. None came, nor was he given any suggestion of being pursued as he moved away from the building with all the speed he could muster.

Slowing down to avoid arousing suspicion when he considered he was well clear of the potentially dangerous vicinity, the Creek made plans for his future. He would return to the Grimsdyke Temperance Hotel to collect everything that might allow himself to be traced. Then he would quit Mulrooney and leave his surviving associates to their own devices. Furthermore, once he succeeded in returning to the safety of the East, he had no intention of continuing to be actively involved in the scheme that had already placed him in such grave danger.

*   *   *

Watching what was happening on the roof across the street, Dusty Fog made no attempt to use the Colt he was holding when the figure shouting in an unknown tongue came into view. Even as he was concluding that Freddie Woods had had success with the Holland & Holland, offering a chance of a prisoner being taken to be questioned about the ambush, he heard the crash of a revolver shot. Although the red glow of the muzzle blast indicated the position from which it was fired, the signboard concealed whoever had done so.

There was no need for the small Texan to wonder who had been the latest target. Seeing the already staggering and clearly wounded man jerk on being hit by the bullet, then plunge over the edge to the street, supplied the answer. Coming to his feet, Dusty intended to change position in the hope of at least discovering who had fired the shot. Before he could move, his attention was diverted from the building.

"Look!" Babsy Smith shrieked, but there was elation and not concern in her somewhat strident Cockney tones as she pointed. "It's Lon and he's all right!"

"He is, thank God!!" Freddie exclaimed, turning her gaze in the direction indicated by the little blonde and inadvertently lowering the rifle.

Despite being aware that the danger from the opposite roof might not yet be over, Dusty suspected the shooting of the wounded man was a prelude to flight on the part of whoever had done it, and he too did as requested by Babsy. There were a number of people on the street below, but he had eyes for none of them. A similar surge of relief assailed him over what he saw.

Coming from the alley into which he had been carried by Mark Counter, the Ysabel Kid was bareheaded. Supported by the blond giant's right hand resting on his shoulder, he was walking a trifle unsteadily. However, he was showing no signs of being injured in any way. Carrying the Kid's black hat, the leather band from around its crown, and the doctor's bag, Doc Leroy was bringing up the rear.

"I'm going down there, honey!" Dusty announced, lowering the hammer of the Colt onto the safety notch between two chambers of the cylinder and tucking it into his waistband. "Watch the roof, there's still another jasper on it. Yell if you see him!"

"If I see him, I'll *shoot,*" Freddie corrected, returning her attention to the other building. "He can do the yelling!"

Grinning at the spirited response, which he knew was in part caused by a relief similar to his own on discovering the Kid was apparently unscathed, the small Texan climbed over the guardrail of the veranda. Calling a warning, he lowered himself as far as possible and dropped the rest of the way. Alighting upon the street, he ignored the excited questions from various onlookers and hurried toward his companions. While doing so, he noticed that Town Marshal Kail Beauregard and three deputies were approaching on the run.

"I'm not complaining because I was wrong for once, mind," Dusty declared, without waiting for the peace officers to arrive, as he halted in front of the other three Texans. They all knew the depth of true feeling beneath the seemingly callous words. "But I'd have sworn I saw you get shot in the head, Lon."

"I thought the same, only no such luck," Doc claimed, before the Kid could speak. Again there was genuine relief obvious to men who knew him as well as did his companions. Holding forward the hat and its band, he showed that a piece was missing from the latter. "Thing was, he got luckier than *anybody,* even a part-Comanch' Texan, has any right to be. The bullet hit the buckle and glanced off, 'stead of going into his fool head respectably."

"So he wasted time on me, 'stead of looking for the buckle," the black-dressed Texan complained. "But what could you expect from a jasper's rides for the Wedge?"

"You're lucky it bounced off your fool head, it might've hit somewhere that could be damaged," Dusty asserted, reaching for and grasping his *amigo'*s right hand in a way that gave the lie to the comment. "Howdy, Kail. Waco took off after the feller's shot Lon, but there could be another of them on the roof across from the Fair Lady."

"Go take a look, Will, Edgar!" commanded the marshal, to whom the last sentence had been directed. "What's it all about, *amigo*?"

"I wish I knew," the small Texan admitted. "Freddie winged one jasper on the roof and another up there shot him. He's lying on the street."

"I noticed," Beauregard replied. "Take a look at him for me, will you, Doc?"

"I just knew I'd get asked!" the Wedge trail hand protested, walking forward. "God damn it, one of these days, somebody'll get shot and I *won't* get asked to tend to 'em!"

"Then you'll start complaining because you've been ignored," the marshal answered.

"He won't be telling you anything," Doc concluded, after examining the body sprawled on the street. "The bullet wouldn't have killed him, but he's broke his neck."

"Do you recognize him, Dusty?" Beauregard inquired, unaware of the relief felt by three spectators on hearing the Wedge trail hand's diagnosis.

"Never saw him before," the small Texan decided. At that moment, guns began to roar some distance away. "Sounds like Waco's caught up with the jasper who tried to shoot Lon."

"Sounds that way," the marshal agreed. "Let's go see. Tend to things here, Tom."

"Take Lon into the Fair Lady, Mark!" Dusty instructed. "Carry him there, should you have to."

"Ain't no call for that," sniffed the Kid, accepting he would slow down his companions in his present far from steady condition. "I know when I'm not *wanted*!"

"Good for Boski!" Kevin Roddy said, *sotto voce,* watching Dusty and Beauregard hurrying away. "He made sure Budapest couldn't talk. Let's hope he and the other two have got away."

"We need more than just *hope!*" Walter Johnson spat back, no louder. "Let's go and make sure they have. Because, if any of them gets taken alive, I don't intend to be anywhere within miles of Mulrooney once they start telling everything they know."

7

THEY CALLED THEMSELVES "BOHEMIANS"

"*Look,* you stupid bastard!" Peter Romanov spat out breathlessly, skidding to a halt and swinging a furious gaze at his companion. "There's no way through he—"

"A *wall,* God damn it!" Rudolph Petrovich was saying at the same instant, also stopping as he too realized there was no other choice. Turning a similarly accusatory glance at the man by his side, he continued just as heatedly and with equal evidence of feeling the strain of their mutual exertions. "Why the hell did *you* bring us down here?"

"*Me?*" the Yakima yelped indignantly, breaking off his angry declaration as an understanding of what had been said by the other Indian struck him. Making a belligerent gesture with his Winchester Model of 1873 rifle, he continued, "It was *your* God damned idea to come this way!"

"Don't try to lay the blame on *me,* you asshole!" the Onondaga warned, accompanying the words with a threatening motion from the Colt Cavalry Model Peacemaker revolver he was carrying in his right hand. Possessed of an identical desire to exculpate himself, he asserted with no greater justification, "It was *you* who turned in here *first*. I just followed you."

Unlike the two conspirators on the roof opposite the Fair Lady Saloon, Romanov and Petrovich had not lingered after having carried out their part in the intended assassination of Dusty Fog and the Ysabel Kid. Nor had they been required to do so according to the instructions upon which they were acting. When assigning them to their duties, aware that being at street level would render them more readily accessible for reprisals, Walter Johnson had stressed the necessity for an immediate and hurried departure as soon as they had done what was required of them. Therefore, having seen the black-clad Texan was hit by the shot that the Yakima had fired at him, they had retreated without making any attempt to ascertain whether or not he had sustained a fatal injury.

Finding they were being followed, the pair had decided against acting upon the rest of the advice given by the New Englander. It had been his suggestion that, once away from the alley, the Winchester at least should be discarded and, as to do so would be less likely to attract unwanted attention, they should walk instead of running. Without having indulged in any discussion, they had mutually concluded that either to slow down or divest themselves of their weapons would be most unwise. However, in spite of having retained the Winchester and revolver, they had had no intention of stopping to try to frighten off or kill their solitary pursuer.

Not only had Romanov and Petrovich realized that to halt and fight would offer an opportunity for the local peace officers to arrive and join in the fray, but neither had forgotten the grim warning given by Johnson. He had claimed that all the men likely to be in the company of their intended victims, even the one coming after them, were exceptionally

competent gunfighters. While neither would have made the
admission openly, they were conscious of their own limitations along such lines. What shooting they had done previously had been restricted to motionless and harmless paper
targets. Each was disinclined to face the risks attendant on
tangling with the Texan, his youth notwithstanding, who was
sticking to their trail with grim persistence.

By taking a roundabout route to the Grimsdyke Temperance Hotel, although it was through a section of Mulrooney
they had not previously traversed, the two "Bohemians" had
hoped to lose their pursuer without the need for a confrontation. Having led sedentary lives in the East, continuing
their hurried flight was calling for much greater physical
effort than either had ever had to exert. Hoping to throw the
dogged pursuer off their track, they had turned a corner
while he was out of sight and discovered the way was
blocked by the wooden wall. It was too high to be climbed
quickly, particularly in their close-to-winded condition, and
it extended to the building on either side without any sign of
a gate. To make matters worse, there was nothing in the *cul-
de-sac* behind which they might hide.

Regardless of the extreme gravity of the situation, neither
Romanov nor Petrovich could resist trying to blame the error of judgment upon his companion!

However, the recriminations were short-lived!

Even as the pair were speaking and turning away from the
wall, they heard the footsteps of their pursuer approaching
from nearer than they had expected!

Then a light came on and the Indians saw the shadow of
the blond youngster starting to appear beyond the corner of
the building around which they had come!

A surge of relief flooded through each "Bohemian" as
they arrived at an identical conclusion. In spite of the high
regard in which Johnson apparently held him, the young

Texan clearly failed to appreciate the danger in which he was being placed by the light to his rear. Not only was the black silhouette being thrown ahead giving a warning of his presence, it was allowing them to ascertain his exact position in relation to themselves. Oblivious of this, he was continuing the reckless advance and would soon be in view beyond the end of the building.

Exchanging glances, Romanov and Petrovich raised and lined their respective weapons at the corner!

In preparation for opening fire, two forefingers tightened upon triggers!

Quivering with anticipation, which was three parts fear for the consequences of failure, the Yakima and the Onondaga watched the shadow lengthening. Although neither had ever heard the term, each was in the state of nervous tension known to hunters as "buck fever" because it frequently afflicted budding sportsmen awaiting the first sight of their quarry. Romanov had already experienced a similar sensation while he was lining his rifle at the Ysabel Kid. However, it was now greatly intensified by the much closer proximity of his latest human target and the realization that he no longer had the benefit of his presence being unsuspected by the intended victim. Not that, he told himself in an attempt to steady his shaking hands, the Texan was showing signs of being alarmed or deterred by the knowledge.

More of the shadow was coming into view!

Another two strides should carry the blond youngster past the corner!

At most, only one more step was needed!

"Now!" Romanov shouted—reverting to his native Yakima tongue in the stress of the moment—an instant before he considered the final stride would be taken by the Texan, wanting to ensure that his companion fired at the appropriate moment and did not leave everything to him.

"Kill him!" Petrovich yelled simultaneously—just as inadvertently speaking Onondaga—and, having just as little faith in the other Indian to assess the situation correctly, impelled by the same motive.

Although the throes of "buck fever" had caused each "Bohemian" to employ his native tongue, which the other did not understand, the exclamations produced the desired effect. Both instantly completed the pressure on the triggers of their weapons. Released from the sears, the hammers of the rifle and revolver snapped forward and the shots rang out at the same instant.

However, the anticipated target had not arrived where the bullets were being sent!

Unfortunately for Romanov and Petrovich, their intended victim had been fully alert to the danger caused by the shadow that was preceding him!

Johnson had been correct in the warning he had given with regard to Waco!

Ever since he was big enough to hold and fire one, the blond youngster had been using firearms. He had received much valuable advice from such acknowledged masters as the Washita curly wolf, Clay Allison, Mark Counter, and Dusty Fog and had acquired considerable practical experience in all aspects of gunfighting. Therefore, he was far from being the unthinking and reckless victim that the waiting pair expected. While aware of the peril created by the light to his rear, he had also seen he might be able to turn this to his advantage.

Instead of continuing to run until in view of the men in the *cul-de-sac,* timing the movement with the knowledge that his life depended upon its accuracy, Waco spiked the high heel of his descending boot into the ground. Performing one of the functions for which his footwear was designed, this allowed him to avoid passing beyond the shelter offered by the building. Even as he was bringing himself to an abrupt halt, he heard the shouted words. The crashes of the rifle and revolver followed too quickly for him to realize these had not been spoken in English. However, not only did the bullets pass harmlessly in front of him to end their flight in the wall at the opposite side of the alley, but the glow from the muzzle blasts allowed him to estimate the positions of his would-be killers.

Listening to what he assumed correctly to be startled exclamations from inside the *cul-de-sac,* Waco was not aware that two different languages were being used. Concluding that he was up against "foreigners" of some kind, he resumed his briefly interrupted advance without taking time to wonder from which country they might originate. Thrusting himself from behind the building, putting to use the information he had acquired, he turned his torso and started swinging his Colts in the directions that he had deduced would point one at each of the men he was chasing. On the five-and-a-half-inch-long barrels ceasing their horizontal arcs, being aimed at just over waist level and by instinctive alignment, the right-hand weapon roared. An instant later, its mate was also discharged.

Discovering he had made the mistake of firing prematurely, the blame that Petrovich started to lay upon Romanov in his native tongue was brought to an end by the .45 bullet that ripped into the center of his throat. Commencing a similar accusation in the language of his race, the Yakima was prevented from completing it by the second piece of conical lead entering his left breast to slash through his heart. Turning away from his companion, who was also being spun around, he allowed the Winchester to fall from his hands and followed it to the ground.

Sent reeling into the corner of the wall and left-side building, blood gushing in a flood from his injury, the Onondaga neither fell nor dropped his revolver. Held erect, if crouching, he gurgled what would have been hate-filled words if the bullet had not cut his vocal cords along with the veins and arteries of his neck. Grasping the butt with both hands, he exerted his failing strength in an attempt to raise and cock the revolver.

On the point of acting as was dictated by his training as a gunfighter, by continuing to shoot on finding himself confronted by a wounded adversary who still retained a weapon and showed signs of meaning to try to use it, the blond youngster refrained. Mindful of the desirability of taking a living prisoner to be questioned, he darted toward the crouching figure. Watching the long-barreled weapon, he was ready to take any evasive action that might prove necessary. However, none was required. Before he arrived, or it could be lined at him, the man crumpled and the Colt slipped from hands that were suddenly inoperative.

Coming to a halt, without the need for conscious thought the youngster took the precaution of kicking aside the revolver discarded by the feebly moving figure crouching huddled in the corner. While he was turning his attention to the other would-be assailant, he heard footsteps approaching from his rear and a moving glow of light improved visibility in the *cul-de-sac*. Glancing over his right shoulder, he identified the two armed men coming from the alley as the owner and chief clerk, the latter carrying a lantern, of the freight outfit. They were acquaintances from his days as a peace officer in Mulrooney and the recognition was mutual.

"It's you, Waco!" greeted the taller of the newcomers, lowering the shotgun he was holding in a position of readiness. "From the look of things, I'd say you've found yourself a mite of trouble."

"If it isn't trouble, it'll do me fine until some real trouble comes along," the youngster replied, returning the Colts to their holsters as he was satisfied there would no longer be any need for them. "That jasper with the rifle gunned down the Kid."

"The hell you say!" the owner of the freight outfit growled. There was genuine sympathy in his voice as he continued, "Was he hurt bad?"

"I didn't wait to find out afore I came after them," Waco admitted and, with the urgency of the situation over, the deep concern he had been holding in check began to well up. "Can you get the doctor fetched *pronto,* Whit? This one's still alive and might be able to tell us why them and some more were laying for Dusty 'n' Lon."

* * *

"They're both cashed in," Doc Leroy reported, having conducted a thorough examination of the two men shot by the blond youngster in the *cul-de-sac.* Knowing the local doctor had left town to visit a patient, Town Marshal Kail Beauregard had asked him to perform the task. It was made easier by the owner of the freight outfit, who anticipated the need and sent for extra lanterns before they arrived. "And, even if the one in the corner hadn't bled to death quicker than anybody could have stopped it, he couldn't have done any talking shot in the throat like he was."

Respecting the members of Ole Devil Hardin's floating outfit for the part they had played in establishing law and order during the vital formative days of Mulrooney, the owner of the freight business had had no qualms over doing as Waco had requested. Having sent his clerk with the message for the doctor, knowing the close bonds between the Texans he had offered to keep watch over the wounded man without needing to be asked. Filled with anxiety over the well-being of the Ysabel Kid, the youngster had been grateful for the suggestion. Satisfied everything was in good hands, he had set off for the Fair Lady Saloon. Before covering half the distance, he was met by Dusty Fog, the slender Wedge trail hand, the marshal, and two deputies. Relieved to hear that his black-dressed *amigo* was not seriously injured, he had guided them back to the scene of his encounter with the would-be killers. On the way, he had described what had taken place and expressed his hope of obtaining information from the wounded survivor.

"I'm right sorry I wasn't able to take at least one of 'em alive, Kail," Waco apologized, after Doc had given his report. "Trouble being, knowing where they'd gone, I figured they was like' to come bu'sting out, heads down and horns a-hooking, when they found's how they'd run themselves into a blind canyon. So I reckoned they'd best be stopped where there wasn't nobody else around to get hurt in the fussing. Only, what with the poor light 'n' all, there wasn't no chance of doing any fancy shooting's'd've let me bring them in just hurt."

"You did what needed doing," Beauregard asserted, satisfied that the blond youngster would have taken both men prisoner if granted an opportunity. "And, even though I likely shouldn't say it according to how some people think, I'd sooner they was taken out this way than left able to start a shooting fuss that could've seen innocent bystanders taking lead." Turning his attention from Waco, he went on, "Do you know either of them, Dusty?"

"No more than I did the one lying on the street across from the Fair Lady," the small Texan replied, once again looking at the two supine bodies.

"Would you have been having trouble with any other spread, Cap'n Fog?" inquired the youngest of the deputy town marshals, being a keen student of the literature giving instruction in the fast-growing subject of deductive reasoning.

"None that's bad enough for them to come after us with

guns," Dusty answered, knowing what was behind the question.

"They're not cowhands, no matter how they're dressed," Waco claimed, indicating the footwear worn by his victims. "Those aren't cowhand boots. Top of which, I'd say they was foreigners of some kind. Leastwise, it wasn't English they started talking when they found I hadn't run out so's they could shoot me."

"That don't mean they was fresh come from off a boat from Europe, though," Doc objected, despite guessing the youngster had reached a similar conclusion. "A lot of folk who didn't come from England are like' to talk the language of their old country when they get het up or spooked. I'll give you one thing, though. It's not only their boots. Their hands are way too soft for them to be working cowhands."

"I wouldn't say they was hired guns, either," Waco declared, willing to concede that the first point raised by the Wedge hand was valid. "Had they been, both of them'd've been toting Winchesters."

"Hi there, Tom!" Beauregard greeted, before the discussion could be continued, seeing the oldest of his deputies coming through the gathering crowd of spectators. "I thought you was off someplace with Chow Willicka fighting the Battle of Chapultepec all over again."

"Could be I'm apple polishing, or bucking for promotion," the elderly peace officer replied. He had been having a celebration with the cook of the Wedge and a couple more companions who had served in the Mexican War. On hearing the shooting he had come to see if his services would be required. Ambling forward, he looked at the bodies and went on, "It's two of *them*, huh?"

"You know them, Tom?" Dusty inquired.

"Not to go up 'n' say 'Howdy' to 'em by name, Cap'n," the

newcomer admitted. "But I was on depot watch when they come in."

"How many of them arrived?" the small Texan asked, aware that Beauregard had continued the policy he originated of having deputies at the railroad depot when trains came in to keep watch for undesirable visitors.

"Four," the elderly deputy answered. "I thought, first off, they was Injuns. Only they called themselves 'Bohemians' when they checked in at the Grimsdyke."

"Bohemians, huh?" the marshal said pensively. "That's a country in Central Europe, from what I remember. Didn't you have some fuss a while back with a bunch from around thereabouts who were trying to get rid of their king, Dusty?"

"Not from Bohemia itself," the small Texan corrected. "It was Bosgravnia and he was their Crown Prince, not a king."

"Did you get all the crowd who were after him?" Beauregard wanted to know.

"There were two different bunches in on it," Dusty answered. "We took out all we knew to be over here."

"Maybe some of their *amigos* are after you looking for evens?" the marshal suggested. "If so, they could've hired help from Bohemia. Except, before anybody asks me, that don't explain why they'd come to Mulrooney instead of Texas looking for you."

"Unless whoever hired them figured we'd be bringing a herd here," the small Texan offered. "So they were told to start looking at Mulrooney, then head south along the trail if we hadn't come."

"We could maybe find the answer at the Grimsdyke," Beauregard asserted. "Would you like to come along, Dusty?"

"*Gracias,*" the small Texan assented, having hoped the offer would be made.

Leaving his deputies to arrange for the bodies to be taken

to the undertaker, the marshal set off with the Texans. However, before they reached their destination, they saw flames rising and heard a commotion. Hurrying onward, they found the second floor of the Grimsdyke Temperance Hotel was rapidly being consumed by a fire. If they had gone around the building, they might have seen Walter Johnson hurrying away.

8

COWHANDS AND DUDES DON'T MIX

"Good morning, Captain Hart, Captain Fog," Walter Johnson greeted, coming to the table at which the trail boss of the Wedge and the small Texan were seated in the Fair Lady Saloon. Then, glancing at the remains of what was clearly their lunch before them, he continued amiably, "I suppose I should be saying, 'Good afternoon.' We city dwellers don't rise as early as we should, I suppose. Am I interrupting anything?"

"Nothing important," Stone Hart replied. "Pull up a chair and join us for coffee. Or would you prefer something stronger and a meal?"

"Coffee will be fine, sir, and I've already eaten at the hotel," the New Englander declared, pulling out and sitting on a chair. "May I ask if anything further has developed with regard to the attempt on your life last night, Captain Fog?"

"Nothing that helps a whole heap," Dusty admitted. "It seems likely the fire at the Grimsdyke was mixed in with the try at Lon and me, but I'm still no closer to knowing why those jaspers came after us in the first place."

"I'm sorry to hear that," Johnson claimed with what appeared to be genuine sincerity, although the opposite was the case.

The last thing the New Englander wanted was for either the small Texan or the local peace officers to discover why the abortive ambush had taken place!

Having been a criminal since childhood, Johnson had learned early that one of the best ways to keep out of trouble with local law enforcement agencies was to study their way of working. Being aware that the enterprise upon which he was currently engaged was far from legal, he had continued to take this precaution on coming to Mulrooney. Knowing of the "depot watch" duties carried out by the deputies serving under Town Marshal Kail Beauregard, he had been able to envisage the full extent of the danger caused by the way in which Hugo Budapest was killed. He had felt certain the arrival of the four young Indians had not gone unnoticed by whichever peace officers were present when they came in on the train, and he was equally convinced that, their physical appearances being sufficiently distinctive to have aroused interest, steps would have been taken to discover where they had found accommodation and who they claimed to be. Therefore, even if their pretense of being immigrants from Bohemia had been accepted, the marshal was sure to go to the Grimsdyke Temperance Hotel with the intention of questioning the other three.

Standing in the crowd that had gathered outside the Fair Lady Saloon after the failure of the ambush, much to the New Englander's relief, he had heard nothing to suggest that any of the deputy marshals accompanying Beauregard had been on the depot watch duty when the "Bohemians" had arrived from the East. Nevertheless, he had also appreciated that it was only a matter of time before the identification was made. Having no doubt that Ivan Boski would try to obtain leniency by implicating himself, Kevin Roddy, Francis Morrell, and the other Indians if arrested for the murder of Budapest, Johnson had known this must not be allowed to take place. He had further realized that he alone must prevent it.

Considering it would be highly unwise to trust even his two white associates more than was absolutely necessary, particularly where the far from legal measures that would be required to ensure the silence of the Creek Indian were concerned, the New Englander had not mentioned his full intentions to either of them. Instead, he had claimed that he was going to make sure the rest of the "Bohemians" did not fall into the hands of the local law as a result of Budapest having been killed in such a fashion. He had countered a suggestion that either Roddy or Morrell should accompany him by pointing out they would be more usefully occupied if they remained in the crowd and listened for anything suggesting there were further developments that might put them and the scheme in jeopardy. Although he had suspected that the possible threat to themselves, rather than their enterprise, was the primary consideration, for once they had yielded to a suggestion he made without argument.

Caring little for what might have motivated the acceptance, being grateful that it had happened, Johnson had set out alone for the Grimsdyke Temperance Hotel. He had been relieved when he had not heard anything to indicate that the peace officer sent by the marshal to investigate the rear of the buildings opposite the Fair Lady Saloon had seen, caught up with, or even only chased and lost Boski. When the shooting had commenced from a different direction, he had concluded that the same did not apply where Peter Romanov, Rudolph Petrovich, and their young pursuer were concerned. He had also deduced, from revolvers having been used after the rifle and another handgun were fired, that the Yakima and the Onondaga had missed the blond Texan.

The Winchester had remained silent after its single discharge, so the New Englander had decided that Romanov must have paid the penalty for a lack of accuracy. As there was no further shooting of any kind, remembering what he had heard about Waco's ability as a gunfighter, Johnson had assumed the same might apply to Petrovich. Being convinced they would prove just as lacking in loyalty as Boski, Roddy, or Morrell, if captured, he hoped that neither was taken alive, able to answer questions. Considering he had no other choice, regardless of whether they talked or not, the New Englander had elected to make the most of whatever time was being granted to him before a deputy who had been on the appropriate depot watch duty arrived to identify the "Bohemians." He decided to continue with his original plan.

Arriving in sight of the Grimsdyke Hotel, Johnson had discovered that he had approached faster and by a more direct route than the man he was seeking. Waiting until the Creek had gone inside through the rear entrance, the New Englander had followed him upstairs and into his room without either of them having been seen by anybody else on the premises. It had come as no surprise to Johnson when he was told that Boski had flight from Mulrooney in mind. Putting to use his considerable skill as a confidence trickster, such being his specialized field of criminal endeavor, the New Englander had lured the Creek into a sense of false security by apparently being in complete agreement with his decision to leave and drop out of any further plans organized by Johnson.

Knowing the chances of a successful escape were practically nil where a man so inexperienced and of such a distinctive appearance was concerned, Johnson had prepared, and had on his person the means by which the would-be deserter could be eliminated. Although he had not been armed when meeting the Texans for the first time, aware of their ability to detect such things and wishing to avoid arousing suspicion, he had felt the need for a weapon might arise when he was unable to dissuade his fellow conspirators from trying to kill Dusty Fog and the Ysabel Kid. A thrust into the kidney region with the gambler's push-knife he had drawn from its place of concealment up the left sleeve of his jacket had toppled the Creek dying to the floor, unable to raise an outcry.

With Boski dead, listening all the time for any indication that the marshal had learned where the "Bohemians" could be located and had come in search of the survivor, Johnson had made preparations to dispose of anything they might have in their belongings that could lead to him. Although it had never been one of his regular sources of illicit income, he had engaged in a couple of swindles involving arson and had known how to produce the result he required. Using stuffing from the mattresses and kerosene out of the lamps as the main fuel, he had set off a blaze in both rooms rented by the Indians—a skill he had acquired at picking locks during his criminal career having given him access to the second —which he had felt sure would destroy whatever evidence there might be of his connection with them. Having waited until satisfied that each fire was going well enough to ensure the desired conflagration, he had once again departed from the premises without anybody other than his now dead confederate knowing he had paid the visit.

On rejoining Roddy and Morrell at the Fair Lady Saloon, much to his satisfaction, the New Englander had been informed that neither Romanov nor Petrovich had lived through their encounter with the blond youngster. In return, Johnson had told his two surviving associates that he had arrived at the Grimsdyke Temperance Hotel to find the second floor was burning and, although he had not seen Boski, believed the fire had been started in the rooms occupied by the four Indians with the intention of destroying their property before it could be examined by the marshal. He had further asserted that, in his opinion, the conflagration had had such a hold before being discovered that no evidence would be left.

Being unaware of the New Englander's cold-blooded readiness to kill when necessary, or of his previous involvements with arson, the two young Easterners had accepted his story. Nevertheless, as they too had believed the Creek would betray them if arrested in the hope of saving his own neck, their sole concern had been that he might be captured by the local peace officers, and they had stated their intention of leaving Mulrooney before this could happen.

While the New Englander would have been quite content to part company with Roddy and Morrell under different circumstances, in view of the way in which the situation had developed he considered it was now imperative they stay together. Their selection to accompany him had been made by the principal financial backers of the scheme, to whom they were closely related, without even having asked whether he was in agreement. Therefore, feeling sure the wealthy Eastern liberals who controlled the purse strings would not otherwise prove any more loyal or trustworthy in a crisis than his present companions, he had seen the advisability of taking precautions to ensure their continued support. If the truth about the fire at the Grimsdyke Temperance Hotel should be discovered, being able to claim that the pair had been willing accessories before and after the fact would render it extremely unlikely their kinfolk—afraid of being implicated in turn—would try to disassociate themselves from him. Rather they would do everything possible to help him reduce, perhaps even evade completely, the consequences of what he had done partially on their behalf.

Such had been their state of alarm, it had called for all Johnson's powers of persuasion to prevent the two young Easterners from immediately taking flight. It was only by pointing out there was no train in either direction that night, then warning of the dangers of trying to leave by some other means of transportation, that he had induced them to agree to wait at least until the following morning. He had strengthened his argument by pointing out how trying to rent a rig, or saddle horses, at such an hour would arouse suspicion and lead to questioning during which their connection with the "Bohemians" might be established. Faced with such a possibility, they had given grudging concurrence to his suggestions. Having gained this, he had explained how he was hoping to turn the introduction to Dusty Fog and the Ysabel Kid to advantage. Nor had he been lying on that matter. It had been one of the factors he had taken into consideration when deciding Boski must be silenced, and subsequent developments had shown signs of proving it was correct.

Before the Texans had returned to the Fair Lady Saloon, the New Englander had taken the precaution of sending his companions back to their suite at the Railroad House Hotel. He had been satisfied that he had frightened them sufficiently to ensure they would follow his instructions and stay there. Relieved of the possibility of inadvertent betrayal by one or the other, he had gone to greet Dusty Fog and express congratulations over the failure of the ambush. Conducting the questioning with all his skill, his judgment of human nature had quickly reassured him that his connection with the "Bohemians" had not occurred to either the small Texan or the local peace officers. Nor, as far as he had been able to ascertain, had the truth about their true racial origins been even suspected, much less discovered.

Johnson had been much relieved by what he had discovered and deduced. On rejoining Roddy and Morrell at the hotel, he had not been lying when assuring them there was nothing to fear. However, without telling them the real reason, he had had no intention of taking unnecessary chances. He had decided to use the possibility of acquiring support for the Society for the Preservation of the American Bison from Ole Devil Hardin as an excuse to keep up his association with Dusty Fog. By doing so, he hoped to receive a warning in advance if there were any developments in the investigation that might lead in his direction.

Although the New Englander had set out with the intention of meeting the trail boss of the Wedge and implementing the next part of the scheme, finding the small Texan was also present had offered him what he considered to be an excellent opportunity to kill two birds with one stone. He was pleased that he had decided against bringing Roddy and Morrell with him. Having no faith in either's courage or intelligence, he was relieved by having avoided the danger of them inadvertently giving a hint of the truth to a man for whose intelligence and perception—outside appearances notwithstanding—he had formed considerable respect.

"You said the fire at that Temperance Hotel might have been connected with the men who tried to kill you and the Kid," Johnson continued, his tone suggesting nothing more than a casual interest. "Have you heard whether that was the case?"

"The whole upper floor was burned out and it was still too hot in what was left for a search to be made last night," Dusty replied. "But Kail Beauregard said he'd have it looked over when things cooled down enough."

"That could be why he's coming now," Stone Hart remarked, glancing to where the town marshal was walking through the batwing doors of the front entrance.

"Howdy Dusty, Stone, Mr. Johnson," Beauregard greeted, striding briskly to the table. "I reckon we've found the fourth of those Bohemian jaspers. At least, we found the remains of a body at the Grimsdyke and everybody else who was rooming on the second floor has been accounted for."

"Excuse me for butting in, Marshal," Johnson requested, remembering something he had read about the small Texan in Eastern newspapers, and his manner implied a willingness to help. "But why do you say they were *Bohemians*?"

"That's what they told the desk clerk they were when they checked in," the peace officer explained. "Do you know something about them?"

"Not firsthand," the New Englander lied, but with an air of veracity that was most convincing. "However, before I retired, I used to do a fair amount of business with Polish and other Mid-European immigrants and I seem to remember hearing that Bohemians were highly thought of as hired assassins. As Captain Fog said he had never seen any of them before, perhaps they were following their trade from the old country like so many other immigrants do."

"It could be," Beauregard admitted, giving a nod indicative of gratitude for what he believed was information offered to help forward his investigation. "And, should it be somebody from Bosgravnia looking for evens behind this, Dusty, they'd be more likely to know how to get in touch with Bohemians than Western hired guns."

"Why sure," the small Texan concurred. "The three we downed weren't range-bred stock, that's for sure. *Gracias,* Mr. Johnson."

"It was my pleasure, sir," the New Englander replied, pleased he would not need to direct attention to the supposition that the quartet had been hired by people from the

European country. "And I hope what I said will be of some assistance to you."

"It could be at that," the marshal asserted. "I'll get off a telegraph message to the New York Police Department, Dusty, and ask if they know of any Bohemians working as hired killers over here."

"Do you know Lieutenant Ed Ballinger of the Chicago Police, Kail?" the small Texan asked, before the peace officer could turn away from the table.

"Not personally like you do," Beauregard replied.

"Then I'll come with you and send word to him," Dusty offered, shoving back his chair and picking up his hat. "He might learn something around his jurisdiction, even if those jaspers were brought over from Europe specially, not living and working here."

"I hope my small piece of information will produce something helpful," Johnson remarked, after the two men had left the table and were beyond earshot. He exuded such apparently genuine sincerity that he might have meant the comment. Then his manner changed subtly, showing none of the satisfaction he felt at having achieved such a piece of misdirection, to suggest he was disturbed by what he was about to say. "I've heard from our backers in the Society—"

"And?" Stone prompted, as the words trailed to an end.

"It was something discussed, without any decision being reached, while we were making our plans for how to transfer the buffalo," the New Englander continued, looking ill at ease. "Now the decision has been reached and I don't know how you will regard it when I tell you."

"Tell me and find out," the trail boss suggested.

"Very well, sir," Johnson obliged. "It has been decided, without my being consulted further, that to keep the final destination a secret for as long as possible, we are to have our own men take them there."

"So you won't be needing the Wedge after all?" Stone guessed.

"On the contrary, sir, we need you more than ever," the New Englander corrected. "The men who are coming are all from the East and have had no experience in such matters, even where handling cattle is concerned. Therefore, provided you are willing to do so, we want you to train them to complete the drive and give advice upon how to watch over the buffalo until they are established at their destination." Watching for and failing to detect any sign of how the news was being received, he went on in an apologetic fashion, "I realize this must appear we do not trust you and your men—"

"That doesn't bother me," the trail boss claimed. "But sometimes cowhands and dudes don't mix too well and—"

"And you think this will prove the case with the men who are already on their way here?" Johnson deduced. "I can assure you that none of them are like—shall we say—my present companions, although they will be going along. In fact, from what I saw of those who were suggested as the prospective trail crew, I think you will find they get along with your men all right."

"Uh huh!" Stone grunted noncommittally, although he was willing to concede that the New Englander had drawn an accurate assumption with regard to his misgivings.

"I'm empowered to offer you a substantial bonus for carrying out the training," Johnson declared.

"I won't say 'no' to that," the trail boss replied. "But I reckon we'd best wait until I've looked over these fellers who're coming before I give you a decision on it."

"That is all right with me, sir," the New Englander assented. "They are coming in on this afternoon's train and you can meet them as soon as they arrive."

9
THEY COULD USE
SOME HELP

"There they are, gentlemen," Walter Johnson declared, from where he was standing with Stone Hart, Waggles Harrison, and Johnny Raybold, pointing to a group of male passengers who were descending from the westbound train. "It seems they have anticipated our intentions and arrived ready for riding."

"They're ready for *riding,* I'll admit," the trail boss replied. "But not for working cattle."

"That's true, sir," the New Englander agreed. "However, their attire will suffice until we reach our camp, and they can obtain more suitable clothing before we set out upon our quest. Providing, of course, you consider they will be suitable for what lies ahead. Will they pass muster, do you think?"

"They look all right from here," Stone drawled.

"But you are reserving your judgment until you have made their acquaintance," Johnson assessed. "And most wisely so, sir. Shall we go and greet them?"

"That's what we're here for," the trail boss assented and, accompanied by his companions, he started to walk toward the passengers they were discussing.

Remaining with Stone since their meeting at the Fair Lady Saloon, the New Englander had not heard whether Town Marshal Kail Beauregard had been able to search the ruins of the Grimsdyke Temperance Hotel. While eager to find out if anything was discovered that might endanger him, he had been too wise to display any interest he had in the matter. To help divert his thoughts from it, he had been engaged in making preparations that had arisen as the result of the supposed revision to the plans for transferring the buffalo. Fortune had favored the enterprise. Knowing a rancher who was not intending to bring any more herds from Texas, the trail boss had purchased a *remuda* of horses trained for working cattle, and the other equipment they would need from him. As an aid to maintaining secrecy and commencing the training of the newcomers, it had been decided they would set up camp clear of Mulrooney while awaiting the discovery of the buffalo to be taken to the new location. With this done, they had come to the railroad depot to meet the party from the East.

"Hello, Mr. Johnson," greeted the tallest of the new arrivals, his accent that of a wealthy and well-educated Bostonian. In his mid-twenties, as they all appeared to be, he had reddish-brown hair and ruggedly good-looking tanned features. While also the most powerfully built of his party, he bore himself in a way that indicated he was neither slow on his feet nor clumsy. "Here we are, all raring to go as folks say out here."

"I'm pleased to see you and hear it, Mr. Crayne," the New Englander replied, his manner more affable than when speaking to Kevin Roddy and Francis Morrell. "However, if you can restrain your eagerness to depart for a few seconds,

I would like to introduce you to these gentlemen who are to be your guides and mentors for the next several weeks."

Although finding the general appearance and behavior of the young Easterners satisfying, as they moved forward eagerly to make the acquaintance of his party, Stone was more interested in watching Johnny. He had invited the redhead to come to the railroad depot for that reason. Despite having faith in his own and Waggles's judgment of character, he wanted to see how a member of the crew responded to the newcomers. Knowing how roughly cowhands could treat dudes for whom they had taken a dislike, he was all too aware of how important good relations between his crew and the Easterners would be. In fact, if these were not forthcoming, he doubted whether the driving of the buffalo could be carried out as was required by Johnson. Much to his relief, he concluded Johnny was sharing his sentiments about them.

While strolling along the platform, like his companions, the redhead had studied the newcomers. He had reserved his final judgment about them, but he considered they might not be as bad as his meetings with Roddy and Morrell had led him to expect. Coming to close quarters and watching how they responded to the introductions, he decided they could prove far more congenial and acceptable company than the pair who had accompanied Johnson and were now waiting outside the depot.

There was much about the Easterners to influence the redhead in their behalf. All were tall, with the unmistakable look of outdoorsmen about them. Bronzed and cheerful, their faces were devoid of the self-importance and surly snobbery always shown by Roddy and Morrell. They had on Eastern-pattern riding boots and breeches. Under loose-fitting coats were shirts with open collars, or turtleneck sweaters. Their headwear was a mixture of flat-peaked caps, round-topped and curly-brimmed derby hats, or the kind of

Stetsons that could be purchased on their side of the Mississippi River. None of them wore gun belts, or showed signs of
being armed in any way. However, wise in the ways of the
West, Johnny regarded the absence of weapons as a point in
their favor.

"When do we get started, Captain Hart?" Geoffrey
Crayne inquired, clearly being considered as leader and
spokesmen by the other young Easterners, after the introductions were completed.

"Not for a few days, at least," Johnson put in before the
trail boss could speak, noticing the Bostonian had employed
the military honorific without the slightest hesitation. "Mr.
Raybold has to locate a suitable herd for us—"

"That shouldn't be too hard, nor take too long," Johnny
inserted. "There's still a fair few of 'em left west of here,
once you get away from the railroad."

"Then we all wish you a speedy return, sir," the New
Englander declared. "And, while you are away, Captain
Hart and Mr. Harrison have kindly offered to instruct our
party in all we will need to know when the time comes for us
to take over sole charge of the herd."

"Speaking with the voice of fully qualified inexperience,
I'd say we'll need to be taught *plenty*," Crayne asserted. Then
he waved in an apparently disdainful fashion toward his
companions and continued, "And, considering what you're
going to have to work with, Captain, I can't claim that I envy
you the task."

"I'm game to give it a whirl," Stone stated, after having
waited until the cheerfully derisive protests of the other
young Easterners had died away. "When you see the kind of
knob-heads I've let myself be slickered into taking on for
training in the past, present company *not* excepted, you'll
figure I've done wonders before and'll maybe bring one off
again."

"Do you reckon he meant you, or *me,* Waggles?" Johnny inquired, although the pointed glance directed his way by the trail boss had given an undeniable indication.

"Was I not natural' given to being modest," the *segundo* replied, "I'd have to come right on out and say the boss I'm so loyal and respecting to couldn't've meant *me,* so that just about only leaves *you.*"

"I'm beginning to wonder whether our respected seniors in the Society realize what they have let you young gentlemen in for, mixing with such company," Johnson commented, adopting the lighthearted spirit in which the conversation had developed. He concluded that the remarks passed between the Texans indicated they were at least willing to accept the Easterners on amicable terms. "Nevertheless, as I feel I have a responsibility to your parents to ensure your continued adherence to good and righteous Christian living, I have decided that you must be preserved from the fleshpots and temptations lurking in this apparently fair and unsullied metropolis."

"Do they *really* have fleshpots and temptations lurking here, sir?" Crayne inquired with seeming eagerness. He considered the events in which he had participated made it inadvisable to let it be known he had visited Mulrooney two years earlier.

"Not that I've sampled them firsthand, of course, but I'm afraid they do," the New Englander confirmed, employing an obviously false tone of unctuous rectitude that he felt sure would be well received by the men about him. A glance around assured him that his supposition was correct and he went on. "So Captain Hart, who agrees with me, and I have decided we will make camp some five miles beyond the city limits until Mr. Raybold finds a suitable herd. In that way, not only will you be saved from said temptation and fleshpots, you will be able to commence learning your duties and there will be less chance of our presence attracting undesirable interest."

"We'd arouse even less if we were dressed like cowhands," Crayne suggested, indicating the attire worn by himself and his companions. "I know we wouldn't sound like Texans if anybody talked to us, but we could say we've been sent west by our families to learn all we can about the ranching business."

"I admit I had something of that nature in mind," Johnson asserted. "Although my thoughts were more along the lines of implying your parents had sent you west to keep you from idleness and the temptations of the flesh, by having you subjected to hard work while learning how to earn a living."

"I prefer *my* suggestion, sir," the Bostonian claimed, accepting the version given by the New Englander as the pleasantry it had been. "And, to save time, we could leave our baggage here while Johnny shows us where we can buy what we need, then go out to the camp."

"We can save even more time," the New Englander supplemented. "There's a wagon waiting outside the depot. Load your bags aboard and Mr. Harrison will set off for the camp with it. Horses are waiting for you at the livery barn and, with your purchases made, you can catch up with it along the way. If that meets with your approval, of course, Captain Hart?"

"It's all right with me," Stone confirmed willingly. "And, while you're at it, Johnny, should you run across the rest of the crew, tell them what's doing."

* * *

"Johnny!"

Hearing his name, the redhead halted the tall story he was telling to the young Easterners he was guiding to a general store that held a sufficiently large stock of cowhand-style clothing to fill their needs. One glance at the speaker—a small, close to buxom, and pretty young woman with fiery red hair and the attire of a saloon worker—told him something more serious than a merely friendly greeting was causing her to hurry in his direction.

"What's up, Ginger?" the Texan inquired, as he and his companions came to a halt.

"You'd best come to the Buffalo House real fast!" the saloongirl replied. "There's going to be trouble!"

"What kind of trouble?" Johnny asked, setting off straightaway.

"Silent, Peaceful, and Rusty are there," Ginger explained, after having darted a puzzled look at the party with the redhead, but restraining her curiosity about them and falling into step by his side. "Bunch of gandy dancers've come in with a railroad lamp they say they're going to hang on the front door."

"I've a feeling that could have some special significance, Johnny," Crayne remarked, following with his companions close on the heels of the Texan and the girl.

"It has," the Texan confirmed. "When rust-eaters from a construction crew hang out a lamp that ways, it means they claim the place for the railroad and nobody else can drink there."

"That strikes me as a somewhat *selfish* attitude," the Bostonian claimed, his tone and manner apparently no more than mildly disapproving.

"Knowing those three knob-heads of our'n who're there, that's how they're like' to see it," Johnny drawled, giving no indication of being perturbed. "Who-all's with 'em, Ginger-gal?"

"Nobody but the morning staff," the young woman replied. "And there's close to twenty gandy dancers."

"That means your friends are outnumbered," commented the second tallest of the Easterners.

"You try telling *them* that," Johnny answered.

Even as he was speaking, the redhead reached the front entrance of the Buffalo House Saloon. One glance over the batwing doors confirmed his suppositions. Despite the clearly hostile attitude of the railroad construction workers who formed a rough half circle around them, his three companions were leaning against the bar. Although two displayed open defiance, none were armed. Johnny had no need to wonder how the lack of weapons had come about.

"Well now, gents," Herbert "Peaceful" Gunn was saying, his heavily mustached face doleful and his tone seemingly apologetic. About five feet nine, looking older than his twenty-nine years, he was well-made without being bulky. "Being a man's wants only to live peaceable with everybody, I'd like to get out like you say we've got to. But, seeing as we didn't have our chaps with us, Silent, Rusty, 'n' me've put our gun belts behind the bar and it'd be a mortal sin to ask for 'em back so soon."

"Was we too," Festus "Silent" Churchman went on, producing a volume of sound out of keeping with his size and nickname. While small, he had the stocky build of a pocket-sized Hercules. "These good folks's words here'd think we didn't like 'em no more and we for sure wouldn't want that."

"Here Ginger-gal," Johnny drawled, unbuckling and holding out his gun belt. "Hang on to this for me!"

"Do you know something, gentlemen?" Crayne said to his companions, as the girl accepted the rig and the redhead strolled in an apparently leisurely fashion into the saloon. "Those Texans don't seem to realize they're outnumbered."

"In that case," declared the shortest of the Easterners, "they could use some help!"

"Shall we give it to them?" suggested another of the party eagerly.

"I was just going to say that!" The Bostonian protested

and, feeling certain the saloongirl could be trusted with any property left in her care, swiftly removed his jacket. "Would you keep an eye on this, please, Miss Ginger?"

"Sure," the redheaded woman assented with a suggestion of relief entering her voice as she guessed what was portended by the request. Draping the gun belt over her shoulder and taking the proffered garment, she went on, "I'd be pleased to!"

Shedding their jackets with an equal alacrity, just as convinced as Crayne was that the considerable sums of money in their wallets would be safely watched over in their absence, the other Easterners acted upon her suggestion by placing the discarded garments between Ginger and the wall of the saloon. With this done, they formed up behind the Bostonian to enter the barroom.

Unaware of what was taking place outside, Johnny gazed about him as he strolled in a seemingly nonchalant fashion toward the railroad workers. Knowing the employees of the saloon were sufficiently experienced to expect trouble to erupt, he was not surprised to see the precautions they were taking. Working swiftly, while the bartenders removed bottles from the shelves and dropped sliding wooden shields over the mirror beyond the counter, the girls and waiters gathered the glassware from the tables to be taken to safety. Therefore, the redhead gave the majority of his attention to the forthcoming opposition. Studying them, he selected the largest as their most likely leader.

"This here's a gandy dancer's house, beef-head," announced the man picked out by Johnny, his voice having a pronounced Irish brogue.

"I didn't know that," the redhead replied, with what sounded like meek puzzlement. "There isn't any railroad lamp hanging outside."

"That's only 'cause Cousin Seamus here hasn't got around

to fixing it yet," the spokesman claimed, indicating a smaller and equally Celtic-looking member of his party who was holding the item in question. "But the intent's as good as the deed, so it's getting the hell out of here all you beef-head'sll have to be."

"I can't take the boys out just yet," Johnny declared, but with well-simulated apologetic tones, indicating what a Texan generally considered to be undressed hips. "My gun belt's behind the bar and, as I'm buying it on time, I'll have to fetch it afore we hit the trail."

"Then go and get it," the spokesman authorized, showing more disappointment than satisfaction at the apparent acquiescence. "Let him through there, gentlemen."

"There you are, Raybold!" Crayne called, passing through the batwing doors at the forefront of the Easterners as the redhead was allowed to join the other trail hands at the counter. "I expected to find you loafers idling somewhere like this. Let's be having you outside to fetch our baggage from the hotel!"

"Now just a little minute there!" the biggest gandy dancer protested, eyeing the newcomers with open disdain. Having been raised in a much poorer section of Boston, he had developed an antipathy, exceeding what he felt for Texans, where such seemingly arrogant young members of that city's wealthy society were concerned. "These *gentlemen*—"

"I'll thank you to keep your nose out of things that don't concern you!" Crayne snapped, having deduced the background of the man he was addressing and concluding how best to bring about the development he wanted. Continuing to model his demeanor upon those members of his own class for whom he too felt considerable animosity, he went on, "And I've no time to bandy words with menials!"

"*Menials*, is it?" the burly gandy dancer inquired menacingly, striding forward until he and the young Bostonian halted at just over arm's length. "Sure and seeing's that what you think we are, would yez honor be wanting me to doff me hat to you?"

"It would be appropriate," Crayne asserted, seeming to be expecting some such humble response. "And I'm pleased to see you know your place in the presence of your betters."

"That I do, your honor, that I do!" the gandy dancer replied, knotting and swinging around his massive right fist as he was uttering the repetition of the first three words.

10

GET HER DONE, WEDGE

Expecting to elicit some form of hostile response from the burly gandy dancer, Geoffrey Crayne was ready and well able to counter the method employed. Among his other sporting activities, he had acquired proficiency in the fast-developing style of boxing that relied upon skill at evading as well as delivering blows rather than the toe-to-toe slugging of bare-knuckled pugilism. Therefore, the reaction of his would-be assailant was "telegraphed" to his alert and trained senses.

Ducking as he had been taught beneath the powerful, yet comparatively slow blow, the young Bostonian straightened as it went harmlessly past. Coming up, he sent a left cross to the chin. Swiftly though this moved, it had considerable power behind it. Caught as unexpectedly as he had believed his intended victim would be, the spokesman for the railroad workers was sent staggering a few paces. However, he kept his feet and showed no signs of being seriously affected by the punch he had taken.

"Yeeah!" Crayne whooped, giving an excellent rendition of the traditional Rebel yell, as he struck the blow. Then, trying adequately to sound like a true son of the Lone Star State, he went on in ringing tones, "Show these Yankee rust-eaters whose place they're in, *amigos*!"

Having had their interest diverted by the entrance of the young Easterners, the rest of the gandy dancers had taken their attention from the Wedge trail hands at the counter. They had shared Crayne's summation of how their leader would behave on being addressed in such an overbearing fashion, but were surprised at seeing how his attempt to object physically turned out. In spite of this, noticing the change that came into the newcomer's accent and knowing Texans often appeared in something more fancy than the usual cowhand-style clothing when celebrating, they drew the conclusion he hoped they would from his yelled-out suggestion. Watching their response, the Bostonian hoped that the men his party had come to assist would prove equally perceptive.

Noticing the newcomers had removed and left behind their jackets, Johnny Raybold had guessed the reason immediately. However, there was no time for him to explain the situation to his companions. Nor did he consider there was any need. He felt sure that as Rusty Willis, Silent Churchman, and Peaceful Gunn were aware he had gone to meet the Easterners they were to teach trail driving, they were shrewd enough to match his summations and realize they had allies close at hand. With that in mind, he responded to the exhortation from Crayne.

"Yeeah! Let's get her done, Wedge!"

Yelling his acknowledgment, the redhead pushed himself from the bar. Going for the three nearest gandy dancers as they were returning their diverted attention to his group, he swung both arms upward and out. Receiving the backhand punches, the men at the right and left of the trio were spun around. However, before the third could be dealt with, he responded swiftly to the threat. Driven back against the counter by a right to the jaw, seeing his *amigos* were justifying his faith in their acumen, Johnny brought up and thrust away his attacker with a foot to the chest. By that time, everybody on both sides was either involved or about to be.

In spite of his frequent declarations of possessing a most pacific nature and a desire to avoid trouble wherever possible, Peaceful Gunn was the second of the Wedge into action by a slight margin. Even as Johnny was backhanding the first two, he was advancing to drive a punch into the somewhat Slavic features of the gandy dancer directly in front of him. Although his victim was sent staggering, he was tackled around the shoulders by a Germanic-looking man.

While Rusty Willis was pitching into a railroad worker at the other edge of the group, Silent Churchman too was showing his mettle in no uncertain fashion. Ducking his head, he hurtled forward to butt the chest of the largest of the gandy dancers in front of him. As the man was driven backward, instead of seeking somebody closer to his own size, he turned upon the second biggest. He was less successful this time. Being grabbed by the front of his vest, he was lifted from the floor and received a surging heave that sent him across the room. However, rebounding from the wall into which he was thrown, he charged over to bound onto the back of the nearest member of the opposition.

At the edge of his party, despite the heavy metal railroad lamp offering a potentially effective weapon, "Cousin Seamus" did not offer to use it in such a capacity. Instead, he handed it to a waiter who was hurrying by to escape being caught in the forthcoming hostilities. He asked for it to be put somewhere safe until the Texans had been taught a lesson and it could be hung outside as a warning to others of their kind. Relieved of it, showing a disregard for his size similar to that of Silent, he rushed at the second tallest of the young Easterners who—taking their lead from Crayne— were plunging eagerly into the fray.

For their part, Crayne and his companions soon showed they would prove an asset, not a liability, to the Texans. All were keen participants in various rugged types of sport and, as a result of intercollegiate confrontations, not entirely unused to engaging in fracases of this kind. With one exception, they displayed roughhouse as well as more scientific fistic skill.

The exception had only just returned from five years spent in China where he had become attracted by and received instruction in what he considered the most effective fighting art of that country. Bringing up his hands in the accepted open, finger-crooked fashion, he started to almost dance around as he had been taught was the correct preliminary for an attack. He found the subject of his attentions was far less stricken by awe than the opponents of his bald-headed Oriental monk teachers. Watching him with frank puzzlement for a few seconds, instead of being too impressed to respond, the gandy dancer he had selected as a victim picked up a chair and crashed it against his side. Struck while one leg was raised in a particularly fancy piece of footwork, he was precipitated against a wall and dropped winded to the floor. He was saved from further attack by another Easterner, employing less flamboyant methods, who took on his assailant.

Probably none of the other combatants had noticed it, but the action of "Cousin Seamus" in giving up the railroad lamp set the tone for the rapidly spreading fight. While everybody was soon going at it with vigor and determination, there was no out-and-out viciousness being displayed. Rather they all seemed to be reveling in the opportunity to let off steam and test the mettle of such worthy antagonists. Even the leader of the gandy dancers, whose treatment might have seemed most likely to cause animosity, did no more than bellow, "So you tricked me, did you, beef-head!" more in admiration than anger before rushing at Crayne.

Fists were flying with varying degrees of skill, feet were lashing out, primitive and more expert wrestling was being employed, but clearly without any desire to inflict serious injury. Even, as first happened to the would-be exponent of *kung fu,* the use of chairs as extemporized clubs was not especially dangerous. Like most saloons in towns where the gathering of different working groups made such confrontations likely to take place, the furnishings, while strong enough to stand up to normal use, were not sufficiently sturdy to be effective weapons. Furthermore, due to the staff taking the precaution of removing all the glassware on seeing trouble was likely to occur, there was no danger of anybody being cut as a result of deliberate or accidental breakage. Heaved over the bar, although there were a couple of heavy bung-starters within easy reaching distance as he got up, Silent Churchman did not attempt to arm himself with one before climbing on top and hurling himself back into the fray.

For all the abandon with which they were going at it, the combatants took care to confine the fighting to themselves. Brawling spiritedly, Rusty Willis found they were approaching a saloongirl trying to join her companions on the stairs leading to the first floor. Separating, they allowed her to pass between them and only resumed their interrupted efforts after she was safely by. Elsewhere, sent reeling against somebody, "Cousin Seamus" spun around ready to defend himself from what he expected to be another assailant. Finding he had collided with a waiter, he held back the punch he was about to deliver and spun around in search of a legitimate foe.

Although eager to watch what happened in the barroom, Ginger did not stay by the front entrance. Gathering up the jackets left in her care, she carried them along the sidewalk until she was able to watch through the window. Her decision to move had not been caused by wishing to avoid the people who, having heard the commotion, were coming to be spectators. Knowing the floor manager had sent a bartender to warn whoever was on duty at the office of the town marshal that trouble seemed likely, past experience had suggested to her what action would be taken. Although Dusty Fog had never claimed to be its originator, a method he had employed to end a similar brawl was still put into effect by the local peace officers.

Not long after the girl had attained her new point of vantage, still holding the jackets and Johnny Raybold's gun belt to save them being stepped upon by the other spectators who gathered about her, the event she had anticipated took place. Called out by a deputy marshal, the members of the volunteer fire department who were on watch knew what was expected of them. Even though they were not being required to deal with a conflagration threatening lives and property, they responded with commendable alacrity. The speed with which the two horse-drawn appliances arrived was testimony to their high standard of training acquired at the instigation of Mayor Freddie Woods as their respected Honorary Chief.

Hardly waiting for the vehicles to be brought to a complete halt, each captain began to run out his hose and make for the batwing doors. Behind them, joined by members of the crowd, the crews took hold of the handles on the sides of the large storage tanks. On command, these were worked alternately up and down to send the contents through the pulsating canvas tubes. While less powerful than would have been the case if the main steam-engined appliance had been employed, the manually ejected water was sent out with considerable force to spray over the fighting men. Even those who were not swept from their feet by the deluge quickly lost aggressive tendencies on being soaked to the skin.

"Calf rope!" Johnny Raybold spluttered, giving the traditional cowhand declaration of surrender. "I don't even like water to *drink*!"

"Turn it off!" the leader of the gandy dancers supported, just as loudly. "It's peaceful we'll be!"

"Sure and isn't that the pity's shame," demanded "Cousin Seamus" of Silent Churchman, whom he had found to be a more than adequate adversary of his own dimensions, as they struggled to sitting postures from being washed off their feet. "Can't a bunch of gentlemen be having a quiet and friendly little discussion without some spalpeen sneaking up and squirting water over 'em?"

"These trail-end town knob-heads's all spoilsports," the Texan replied, in a similarly aggrieved tone. "Anyways, seeing's they ain't going to let us go on with our—talk—maybe they'll let us set each other up a drink."

* * *

"Roll out! Roll out! Roll out! If quality folks like me 'n' Joseph Henery there can't sleep, ain't *nobody* at-all, not even good ole General Sammy-well Houston hisself if he was to hand, got the right to lie a-snoring!"

"Come on now! Come on now! Come on *now*! Let's see you-all rolling out from them blankets and suggans, blast your cow-punching hides. The sun's so high, it's like' to burn your eyes out 'n' half the day's gone already!"

Standing near the lowered and supported tailgate of the chuck wagon that was his pride and joy, William Randolph

"Chow" Willicka, cook of the Wedge trail crew, was supplying an accompaniment to the words he was bellowing in a seemingly irate Texan drawl by banging vigorously on the bottom of a frying pan with a butcher's sharpening steel. Short and wiry of build, he was bare-headed and had thinning gray hair. However, while there was grizzled stubble on his leathery brown features, it was only an overnight growth, and otherwise his appearance and attire were clean. His attire was that of a working cowhand, but the white apron he had about his midsection proclaimed his true vocation. There was much about the way in which he bore himself that was reminiscent of an aged, yet still feisty fighting cock.

The vocal support for Chow's tirade was coming from the rear of a similar type of vehicle at the opposite side of a fair-sized campfire. Joseph Henry Abrahams, whose accent was also that of a Texan, was adding to the cacophony by clashing together the bases of two baking pans. Bigger, burlier, with a stature closer to the traditional lines of a cook, he was perhaps half the age of the other noisemaker, from whom he had learned his duties. Knowing him to be competent, trustworthy, and discreet, Stone Hart had recommended to Walter Johnson that he be hired to take care of feeding the Easterners when they parted company with the Wedge.

"Coffee's boiling and grub's a-waiting!" the pair continued in unison, paying not the slightest attention to the protests from the men they were waking up. Laying aside the utensils with which they had added to the commotion, they went on shouting as they made their way to where everything was prepared to serve breakfast. "Come and get it! Come and get it! Come and get it, afore we throws it out for some other hawgs!"

The time was four o'clock in the morning and, regardless of the claim made by "Joseph Henery," the sun was only just starting to raise its first red glow of the day above the eastern horizon.

Disturbed like everybody else in the camp, except those few whose duties were preventing them from sleeping, Johnson threw off the covers and swung his legs to hoist himself into a sitting position on the folding camp bed he had bought in Mulrooney. On account of his age, which was exceeded only by that of Chow Willicka, he alone was not expected to spend the night—as the Texans expressed it—with the ground for a mattress and the sky for a roof. Instead, he was granted the privilege of occupying the third of the four vehicles—two of which he had purchased under the guidance of Stone Hart prior to setting out—forming a rough square and serving as a partial windbreak for the fire upon which the cooks had prepared the previous evening's and this morning's meal.

Almost three weeks had gone by since the New Englander had sought to distract Dusty Fog and Town Marshal Kail Beauregard in the Fair Lady Saloon. To his way of thinking, despite the potential danger caused by the abortive attempt to kill the small Texan and the Ysabel Kid, everything was progressing in a most satisfactory manner. While the death of the four young Indians had caused some revision to the scheme, this had been accomplished without difficulty. Furthermore, he considered the way in which one of them died had produced a beneficial effect for him.

On hearing of Ivan Boski's body having been discovered in the charred ruins of the Grimsdyke Temperance Hotel, Kevin Roddy and Francis Morrell had guessed this was not the result of an accident. Johnson had been too distrusting to admit openly he was responsible, but had pointed out the law would consider them to be his accessories if Beauregard tried to prove he was responsible. The supposition that the man they had regarded as nothing more than a petty criminal, employed to supply knowledge that they lacked, could have committed murder and arson brought a satisfying change in their attitude toward him. Realizing they were dealing with somebody who not only faced the death penalty if their belief was correct, but was able to make them to share his fate, there had no longer been any doubt that he was running things. Instead of the earlier arguments, they had yielded without question to his every proposal.

Making the most of his association with Dusty Fog, Johnson had continued to keep in touch with the investigation. Replies to the queries had come from Lieutenant Edward Ballinger and the New York Police Department. Their sources of information had confirmed the use of Bohemians as hired assassins by various Mid-European countries, but nobody had heard of any being employed in the United States. Despite this, he had soon become convinced that the true motive was not suspected.

While taking the precaution of watching for developments that might place him in jeopardy from Dusty Fog or the local law, the New Englander had seen the scheme going forward smoothly in other directions. As he had promised Stone Hart, the young men brought by Geoffrey Crayne were vastly more satisfactory in character and behavior than Roddy and Morrell. None of the twelve was aware of what was really intended. Instead, they were genuinely interested in the possibility of transferring to an area of safety a sufficiently large breeding stock to save the buffalo from extinction.

Good relations had been established early, when the Easterners had come so willingly to the assistance of the four Wedge hands in the Buffalo House Saloon. It was strengthened when Crayne, claiming he had struck the first blow to start the fight, insisted that he and his group pay more than their fair share to cover the cost of the damages. With this matter settled, no charges had been made against any of the combatants and all had parted, after a cheery celebration, on the best of terms.

The first and most vital problem that had required solving had been to locate sufficient buffalo to meet the needs of the scheme. However, as Stone Hart had promised, this had proved a far from insoluble proposition. While hunting was already decimating the formerly enormous herds, once away from the railroad and people following in its wake there were still a good number of them left. Under the command of Johnny Raybold, in his capacity of scout, members of the Wedge had set off westward to find what was needed.

Before the redhead had sent Doc Leroy and Rusty Willis to report that a suitable herd had been discovered and was being kept under observation, the trail crew from the OD Connected had set off for Texas without changing their belief that their attempted ambush was at the instigation of enemies who lived in Europe and sought revenge for a scheme thwarted by members of the floating outfit in the United States some time before. However, while this point of view was shared by Beauregard, Johnson was not sorry to leave Mulrooney as it reduced the danger of his surviving associates saying something that might lead to the truth being discovered.

Apart from the Easterners improving their horsemanship, hardening riding muscles to stand the strain of long hours spent in the saddle, learning the ways of the Texas pattern rigs they were using, and learning to live on the trail, the journey to the vicinity of the herd had been uneventful. Having shown the least aptitude in all matters, Roddy and Morrell had concurred—albeit with bad grace—when Johnson assigned them to carrying out the menial duties of cook's "louse." Wanting to avoid arousing interest, the party had kept clear of all human habitation when away from Mulrooney and, at last, were ready to find out whether making the drive was possible.

11

WE'RE HEADING FOR TEXAS

Known as a "bed" wagon, the mobile accommodation allocated to Walter Johnson had none of the specialized addi-
tions fitted to the purpose-built vehicles that were the close-
to-sacrosanct domain of Chow Willicka and Joseph Henry
Abrahams. While it would serve as an improvised ambu-
lance, should anybody sustain injuries that precluded riding
a horse, its primary function was to transport hobbles, a rope
for making a temporary corral, a keg of "good enoughs"—
ready-made horseshoes of various sizes to serve as replacements for any lost away from the services of a blacksmith—
other kinds of general gear, and, hence the name, the bedrolls of the crew. However, one item generally carried would
not be needed and was missing. This was the branding iron
with which a conventional trail crew made good losses, or
added to the size of the herd they would be selling, by apply-
ing their mark of ownership upon any "mavericks" encountered along the way.

As he peered through the open flaps of the bed wagon's canopy, after having knuckled open his gummy eyelids, the sight that greeted the New Englander's gaze was probably being duplicated many times between the Rio Grande border of Texas and the railroad towns in Kansas. While the words being bellowed by the cooks and the means employed to supplement the disturbance would differ somewhat, the response from the men they were arousing was likely to be much the same. Unable to continue sleeping, they soon began to extricate themselves from the shelter offered by blankets and thick patchwork quilts, known as "suggans," wrapped in waterproof tarpaulin. On rising, clad in whatever style of nightwear was favored—most undressing being restricted to the removal of hat, bandana, vest, shirt, pants, and boots—some of them extended and flexed their limbs to loosen stiffened muscles. Others favored either scratching at stomachs or running fingers through their hair to massage the scalp. However, no matter what the physical response might be, all joined in heaping verbal abuse against the far from distressed or concerned cause of the disturbance to their rest. It was only when *not* being addressed in such a seemingly hostile fashion that an experienced range country cook became worried. The omission served as a warning, which he had better heed, that his culinary efforts were neither being enjoyed nor appreciated by the other members of the crew.

Thinking of his hopes for the future, Johnson found one aspect of the scene particularly satisfying!

With the exception of Kevin Roddy and Francis Morrell, apart from their accents, the New Englander could discern little difference between the Easterners and the Texans. Nor, he reminded himself, would this state of affairs change too drastically when the men leaving their beds and cursing the cooks had completed their, of necessity, primitive ablutions and donned whatever clothing had been removed the previous night. Although his fellow conspirators had declined to do so, the men sent by the Society for the Preservation of the American Bison had discarded the riding attire they brought from home as unsuitable for the work they would be doing and had fitted themselves with Western-style clothing. They had also supplemented the firearms each had purchased before leaving the East with a gun belt, but had accepted the advice they received and refrained from going armed while in Mulrooney.

Satisfied his dupes would pass as genuine cowhands well enough to avoid adding to speculations as to what they were doing after they had parted company from the Wedge, Johnson stood up. Collecting a towel and dropping from the lowered tailgate of the wagon, clad in the long flannel nightshirt and carpet slippers that had been the subject of numerous jocular comments from the Texans when he had first appeared wearing them, he joined the line waiting to wash in the tub of warm water supplied for that purpose by the cooks. Having done so, leaving a shave until a more convenient time in the evening, he returned to his sleeping quarters to dress in the open-necked tartan shirt, lightweight off-white jacket, tan Stetson with its crown in the style of Texans, Eastern riding breeches, and boots that he had selected as attire suitable to his years and pose as a businessman turned rancher from beyond the Mississippi River.

Like the other Easterners, even Roddy and Morrell, the New Englander had adopted the precaution of upturning and shaking his boots before donning them in the morning as had been advocated by the Texans. He had been informed this was currently less essential than it could be in hotter, more arid regions where scorpions and even rattlesnakes sometimes sought warmth and shelter in discarded footwear during the chill of the night. Knowing they were going into

an area where such an eventuality might occur, although as
yet he had not divulged this information even to the trail
boss, he had considered it advisable to cultivate a habit that
could save him from being bitten by a poisonous creature.
Doc Leroy was not accompanying the party. On arriving in
Mulrooney to report that the buffalo had been found, Doc
had received news of urgent private business that required
him to return to Texas without delay. Therefore, in the absence of such competent medical assistance as would otherwise have been available for at least some of the journey,
Johnson had decided that taking precautionary measures
assumed an added importance.

With his dressing completed, Johnson once again left the
wagon. Strolling to where the two crews were mingling as
they collected their breakfast, he looked for Stone Hart.
Failing to locate the trail boss, he listened to a conversation
that—with slight variations—had become an accepted part
of every morning's activities.

"And what culinary delights await us beneath the covers
this fine morning, would say, Senator Raybold?" Geoffrey Crayne inquired, having firmly established his acceptance by the others—albeit with the thinly concealed disapproval of Roddy and Morrell—as the prospective trail boss
when the time came to separate from the Wedge. "Could it
perhaps be a compote of fresh peaches and strawberries in
whipped cream, baked French toast with marmalade sauce,
rolled bacon strips, and eggs *a la* Rossini?"

"Not *again,* surely, Congressman Crayne?" the red-haired
scout replied, his tone and demeanor registering ennui. Having taken more than one vacation in major Eastern cities at
the conclusion of trail drives, Johnny had sampled all the
delicacies to which the Bostonian had referred. "Why can't
the chef give us good ole boys something real *special* like

whistle berries, fried sowbelly, cackle fruit, and gun-wadding bread for a change?"

"By George, Senator, I do believe he *has*!" Crayne exclaimed, his surprise as well-simulated as the behavior of the Texan had been. He ran a most appreciative gaze over open pans containing pinto beans, sizzling bacon—in slabs rather than daintily rolled strips—and fried eggs, which were awaiting the hungry crews. "And with the added treat of Arbuckle's specially imported, superfine ground coffee and sourdough biscuits no less. Now that is what I call a treat for the gods and it's far too good for these peasants around us."

"Howdy, Mr. Johnson," Waggles Harrison greeted, coming up while the cheerful conversation was taking place. "Looks like we've got a good day for moving out."

"So it does, sir, so it does," the New Englander agreed, allowing the plate he was holding to receive a liberal helping of eggs, bacon, and beans. While collecting a tin cup filled with steaming coffee, a knife, and a fork, he glanced around once more. "Everybody appears to be in most excellent spirits, but I don't see Captain Hart anywhere."

"Told me last night's how he aimed to go and look over the buffalo," the *segundo* of the Wedge replied, also gathering breakfast. Accompanying Johnson toward the bed wagon, he went on, "And here he comes from doing it right now."

"Good morning, Mr. Johnson, Waggles," Stone Hart drawled, joining the two men by the tailgate of the vehicle after having collected a well-laden plate and cup of coffee from the serving tables.

"And a good good morning to you, sir," the New Englander replied. "You put us all to shame by your diligence before breakfast. Is all well with our herd?"

"They're still around and I'll take you out to them when we've eaten," the trail boss answered. "Only I wouldn't go so far as to say they were *our* herd just yet a-whiles. Could be they'll have themselves a few notions of their own when we try to head them up and move them out."

"Talking of which," Waggles put in, "I don't want to sound all nosy and pushy-like, but I reckon it'll be some easier if we know which way you want them fool critters headed afore we even start *trying* to do it."

"By cracky, Mr. Johnson, see what it is to have a right smart *segundo*!" Stone exclaimed, as he and the other Texan swung expectant gazes at the man who had hired them. "Now me, I'd *never* have thought of anything like *that*. Thing being, though, seeing as how it has been thought of, I'd say it's come time for you to start unsealing those 'sealed orders' and let us in on the secret."

"It is, sir, it most certainly is!" the New Englander assented with the joviality that came so naturally when required and effectively disguised his true ruthless nature. "And I thank you for your patience and forbearance in restraining your justifiable curiosity this long."

"I've never seen no sealed orders," Waggles commented. "The Cap'n and me didn't get any when we was riding with General Hood's Texas Brigade in the War and nobody else who-all's hired us since's figured we needed 'em."

"Unfortunately, sir, I'm unable to oblige you in this instance either," Johnson apologized. "You see, when I made reference to 'sealed orders,' it was merely a figure of speech. They were communicated to me verbally before I came west, to be passed on when I considered the time was ripe."

"Was I asked," the *segundo* asserted, but without any suggestion of animosity, "I'd say the time's so ripe now, it's like' to fall offen the tree."

"I agree with you most wholeheartedly, sir," the New Englander declared. Pausing a moment, as if wishing to give an added impact to his next words, he continued, "Gentlemen, we're heading for Texas!"

"Texas?" Stone and Waggles exclaimed at the same instant and in identical tones, exchanging glances closer to surprise than either had ever exhibited before in Johnson's presence.

"Texas!" the New Englander affirmed, not entirely displeased to have provoked so much of a reaction from two men he had hitherto found completely unemotional as far as showing their true feelings was concerned. "While I still am not at liberty to disclose exactly where it is located in your home state, even to you, the Society has obtained a large tract of land and, under the pretense of conducting an experiment into the feasibility of raising a breed of cattle that will yield more and better quantities of beef per head, they are already having it cleared of longhorns and predatory beasts ready for our arrival."

"That sounds like a right smart idea," the trail boss assessed. "And we can understand why the folks in your Society want the place keeping secret, even from us. But Texas covers a whole heap of ground and it'll help us pick out which way to head for the best, so's we can keep as few folks as possible from learning what you're really figuring on doing, if you can narrow it down to a mite less than the whole state."

"Your point is valid, sir," Johnson conceded. "I would like you to take us to the junction of Rita Blanca Creek and the Canadian River. Once there, we can part company and my young men will complete the delivery, then care for the buffalo until they become self-sufficient."

"We should ought to have been able to teach them all they'll need to know by then," Waggles claimed. " 'Cepting for those two Arbuckles you've had trailing along since we first met, they're a pretty good bunch—for Down East Yankees."

"I'm delighted to hear it, sir," the New Englander replied, considering the comment about the men sent to join him at Mulrooney was justified and complimentary. He was also aware, as a result of his association with the Texans, of what was implied by the reference to Roddy and Morrell. "And I'd like to say I picked them all—"

"Even the Arbuckles?" the *segundo* queried in a tone of disbelief, darting a glance to where the pair in question were carrying out their far from demanding duties in as desultory a fashion as they dared. They had been subjected to the caustic tongue of the Wedge's cook on the first occasion he had found them slacking. "Chow reckons's how he wouldn't have taken neither the one of 'em to be even louse for his louse, if he'd been given hand choice on it."

"*Somebody* must love them," Stone suggested dryly, "to have sent them along."

"Or maybe just wanted to see the back of 'em for a spell," Waggles offered.

"The Society made the selection without consulting me," Johnson explained. Wanting to change the subject, as he had no desire to be questioned further about the unsatisfactory pair being chosen, he turned his gaze to the trail boss. "You look somewhat pensive, Captain Hart. Is something troubling you?"

"No!" Stone replied, speaking more sharply than he intended because he had been jolted by being addressed directly from a train of thought he found intriguing. "I reckon we'd best start figuring which trail on the way will let us avoid going any nearer to folks than we have to."

Knowing much about the cattle business in Texas, even though as yet he did not own a spread, the trail boss was trying to envisage where a tract of land sufficiently large for the purposes of the Society had been obtained. Regardless of the enormous area within the boundaries of the state, free space was becoming increasingly hard to acquire. Despite much still being technically "open range," ranchers considered portions of varying sizes—generally defined by physical features such as streams or ridges—as being their respective domains. Almost the only region of any size not considered the property of some rancher or another was the Palo Duro country. This was the territory of the *Kweharehnuh* Comanche. Unlike the other bands of their nation, they had not been persuaded to go onto a reservation and had so far denied the use of their land to prospective cattle raisers.

Before Stone could produce even a theory regarding the possible location of the new home for the buffalo, he was interrupted by the question from Johnson. Nor was he allowed to return to his thoughts on the matter.

"I'd say we should swing southeast and 'round from there," Waggles suggested. "That way, we'll steer clear of the Indian nations. Those red-sticks take a toll on cattle herds going through, which's reasonable enough seeing's it's never over high, but I wouldn't want to take the chance of letting them see buffalo on the hoof."

"A most valid point, sir," Johnson admitted, but he had no wish to continue discussing the possible reaction of Indians to the sight of so many creatures that had once meant a free-ranging way of life to them. "Even should the route you select take longer than going in a straight line, it will allow my young men more time to acquire the skills they will need to deal with the herd after we part company from you."

"The time won't be wasted," Stone agreed, deciding against repeating his already refused suggestion that Johnny Raybold at least should stay with the Easterners during the last stage of the journey. "We'll swing around into North Texas along the trail Colonel Goodnight blazed rather than let himself be forced into paying Uncle Dick Wootten's head tax toll for going through Raton Pass."

"Isn't Raton Pass in New Mexico?" the New Englander inquired.

"It is, unless some Yankee carpetbagger's grabbed it off and took it home with him," the trail boss confirmed. "And so's the trail we'll be following. We're in Eastern Colorado right now. It isn't going to call for too big a swing to go through Northeastern Mew Mexico and miss the Indian nations."

"Top of which," the *segundo* supported, "the trail's not likely to be having herds of cattle on it while we're going through, so we'll find decent water and grazing."

"No offense was intended by my question, gentlemen," Johnson asserted. "You're the experts upon all such matters and I'm entirely in your hands. That way, I'm sure I can escape the consequences if anything goes wrong by pleading insanity."

"Hot damn if you're not starting to think like a Texan!" Waggles grinned.

"Good heavens, so I am!" the new Englander replied, also smiling as he concluded his query had not been taken the wrong way by either the trail boss or the *segundo*. "I really must guard against it becoming permanent."

"Most folks would give their eyeteeth and more to have it happen to them," Stone assured Johnson, so soberly he might have been supplying information of the greatest importance. Then he glanced around and an urgent note came into his drawl. "I know the look we're getting from the cooks. It means, 'Why the hell don't you three get finished feeding like everybody else, so's we can do our chores 'n' get ready for moving out.' "

"Then, in the light of the last month's experience of such matters, I would suggest we eat up," the New Englander replied and started to carry out his suggestion.

"All right, fellers!" Stone called, after having finished his breakfast and deposited his utensils in the pot of hot water provided for washing them. "Time's come for you-all to start earning your pay. Load up and saddle up. We're heading for the herd!"

12

HEAD 'EM UP,
MOVE 'EM OUT!

"That's the bunch Johnny picked out, Mr. Johnson, if it's all right with you," Stone Hart announced, having halted his large blaze-faced bay gelding so that he and the New Englander by his side could just see over the rim of the slope they had been ascending and into the valley below. "There'll be around fifteen hundred head, at a guess, with about the right mixture of mature bulls, mama cows, and young stock to give you the breeding herd you'll need. I know it's more than you reckoned on setting up with, but we're likely to lose some along the way."

"I hear that's even been known to happen with cattle on the trail," Walter Johnson replied, his voice holding its usual mixture of friendly understanding. He was controlling, without undue difficulty, the spirited dun horse that had been allocated to him from the Wedge's *remuda*. Despite preferring to restrict his illicit activities to Eastern cities where public transport was available, he had also earned some of his ill-gotten gains in rural areas where these forms of travel were less available as a means of taking flight should things go wrong. He had therefore considered it advisable to become a competent rider. Since leaving Mulrooney, he had grown accustomed to sitting the low-horned, double-girthed Texas range saddle provided with his mount. In fact, he soon concluded it was far more comfortable than any Eastern rig would have been if used for several hours a day. "And, with the kind of herd you'll be handling this time, there will be little chance of collecting replacements to help you achieve the ambition of every trail boss."

"And what ambition would that be?"

"According to what I've heard, every trail boss leaving Texas with a herd expects to lose a few head and feed beef to his crew along the way, but still hopes to arrive at the shipping pens with at least as many as when he set out."

"You've heard the living truth," Stone confirmed, showing no surprise as he had become used to the New Englander displaying knowledge of Western matters. "And that's what we all try to do, even though we don't always make it. Only this time, like you say, we're not likely to find buffalo along the trail to make up for any we lose."

On receiving the order to get ready for moving out, the Wedge hands and Easterners, to whom instructions on the subject had already been given, had wasted no time. Those who had not already done so quickly finished eating and returned the dishes to be washed by Kevin Roddy and Francis Morrell. Then all, as was expected of them, wrapped and placed their bedrolls in the appropriate wagons. Collecting horses from the *remuda* driven into an extemporized rope corral, they had set off with the trail boss and Johnson, leaving the cooks and two reluctant "louses" to complete breaking camp.

Halting at a sufficient distance to avoid disturbing and

perhaps putting the herd of buffalo to flight, Stone had given the men their final instructions. They had already been paired off, but needed to be allocated duties resulting from the information he had acquired while carrying out his reconnaissance earlier in the day. Using a piece of barren ground, he had drawn a rough map of the area and told each team of a Texan and an Easterner where to position themselves around the animals. Repeating his warning that everybody must remain in concealment until receiving his signal to commence, he had concluded by indicating the point from which it would be given.

Having accompanied the trail boss to their designated position, Johnson had been impressed by the thoroughness with which the arrangements for commencing the drive were made. While forcing himself to carry on the seemingly lighthearted conversation, holding his voice to as low a level as that of his companion despite there being something over a quarter of a mile separating them from their intended quarry, he was studying with great interest the mass of distinctly shaped creatures scattered in front of them.

It was not the first time that the New Englander had seen specimens of the animal so essential to the success of the scheme upon which he was engaged. Since a zoological gardens had been established in Philadelphia in 1859, first Cincinnati and then other Eastern cities had embarked upon similar ventures. Being easy to obtain and keep in captivity, although breeding rarely occurred in such confined conditions, almost all had included buffalo to supplement their more exotic exhibits. He had not visited the "zoos," as they were already being called, because of an interest in the animals on display. Experience had taught him that anywhere that attracted people in large numbers also provided opportunities, of making acquaintances who became victims of his illicit activities.

Gazing into the valley and contemplating his future plans, Johnson began to experience a sensation close to awe. Even at the distance separating them, the buffalo struck him as being much larger than those he had seen through the bars of a cage in a zoological gardens from a much closer range.

"Egad, sir!" the New Englander breathed with, for once, a suggestion of his true feelings tinging his voice. "Having been granted my first view of them *en masse* and in their natural element, I trust that you will take no offense when I say, with all due respect for your knowledge and considerable experience in such matters, that I find it hard to believe even you and your men can hope to compel so many enormous creatures to go where we want them taken!"

"It wouldn't be just *hard,*" the trail boss corrected. "Even granted you've got us Texans trying to do it, it'd be *impossible.*"

"Impossible?" Johnson exclaimed, snapping his attention from the buffalo to the badly scarred face of the man by his side. What he had just heard was at odds with the arrangements for handling the herd that had been made. His long involvement in various types of confidence tricks led him to wonder if he was being set up for a demand to have the payment for the delivery increased. "Are you telling me it *isn't* possible to move them after all?"

"Not exactly," Stone replied soothingly, realizing his comment had been misinterpreted, in spite of his reference to Texans as a means of relieving the tension he had sensed was afflicting the New Englander. "But leave us not forget what I've been warning you ever since we first met."

"And that is, sir?" Johnson inquired, having been impressed by the competence of the trail boss and the confidence shown by the other members of the Wedge crew.

"I can't lay claim to having any knowledge and experience, considerable or otherwise, about handling buffalo on the trail. Nor can any other white man, comes down to a real sharp point. But, surely as night follows day, there's one thing I do know for *certain* about them."

"And what might that be, sir?"

"There's no way we, or anybody else for that matter, can *compel* those buffalo down there to do anything at all, except by stampeding them, which isn't what we need," Stone warned. "So, going by what the Ysabel Kid was able to tell me about them and their ways—and that was only learned by word of mouth from his Comanche kinfolks—all we can do is pray for the good lord to look kindly on us for being *loco* enough to even *try,* then treat them like they was a bunch of brush-popping *ladinos* fresh brought in on a roundup and needing to be trailed."

"Ladinos?" Johnson queried, the word being new to him.

"That's what us Texans call longhorns that have been born and grown up wild in the thorny bush country," the trail boss explained, realizing this was the first discussion he and his companion had had about how he intended to deal with the buffalo. "Any time you find you've got a bunch of them gathered to be taken on the trail, you know all you can do is try to *persuade* them to move whichever way you want them headed because figuring on *compelling* them isn't a lick of use."

"I see what you're driving at, if you'll excuse what must have sounded like a terrible pun," Johnson declared, concluding his fears of an ulterior motive were groundless. He made his next words more of a statement than a question. "And, in the course of your career, you have driven herds of these *ladinos*."

"I reckon I'd be close to justified was I to say 'yes' to that," Stone answered. "Fact being, with the small spreads that mostly need to have us take their herds, I'd say Wedge has handled more *ladinos* than stock that'd been held and winter-fed on the home range. But they're still just cattle, no matter how wild and uncurried they've lived in the thorny breaks. What we've got to find out is whether buffalo, which are natural' born and raised wild critters from back when, can be persuaded, not compelled, to act about the same as *ladinos* do."

"And you think they can be?"

"I wouldn't have taken your money and agreed to give it a whirl if I didn't. It isn't going to be *easy*, that's for sure, but I never could resist a challenge."

"By gad, sir, you're a man after my own heart!" Johnson stated, all his misgiving having gone and the respect he had acquired for the badly scarred Texan restored. Taking out and glancing at his pocket watch, he sucked in a deep breath. The suggestion of drama that came into his voice was genuine as he went on, "And now, sir, the moment is at hand for us to embark upon our project!"

"That it is," Stone confirmed, a similar tone permeating his generally unaffected drawl. "And we'll right soon know whether it can be done. At least, we're going to find out whether we can even get them started moving the way we want them to go."

"Then I trust, sir, you will believe me when I say it is not merely a matter of my personal monetary considerations that leads me to say I wish us every success in our venture," Johnson requested, and still the sincerity of his demeanor was not assumed. "And that, no matter how it turns out, nobody else could have done better in my opinion."

"Gracias," the trail boss responded, looking a trifle embarrassed at the praise. Wanting to lighten the seriousness of the conversation, he continued, "I know it's your herd, but you can't shout, 'Head 'em up, move 'em out!' like they were longhorns. So, if you don't mind taking second best, give Waggles the wave 'round to start them."

"No, sir!" Johnson refused, politely yet definitely, but showing he was not ungrateful for the offer. "While I am pleased to have been accorded the opportunity, that honor must go to *you*!"

Although Stone had set several trail drives into motion since having elected to earn his living in such a fashion, he hesitated for a moment before doing as the New Englander suggested. Never, not even on the first occasion he had given the by now traditional order to "Head 'em up, move 'em out," had he experienced such a strong sense of occasion. He realized that the party he was currently leading was about to engage upon something unique. It might never again be attempted. Even if it should be, in all probability the herd involved would be smaller than the one beyond the rim.

It was upon the acquired facts, imparted to the Ysabel Kid by his Comanche grandfather, that the tactics to be employed on the drive were based. Having formulated his plans based upon considerable experience at handling *ladinos,* in particular while moving them from their home range to Kansas, Stone was gambling on the buffalo behaving in a similar manner. Nothing showed on his scarred features as he waved his Stetson in a circular motion at arm's length above his head, but he was just as eager as the man at his side to discover whether the instructions he had given would produce the desired effect.

* * *

"Looks like funning time's over and we've got to start earning our pay, *amigo,*" Waggles Harrison remarked, speaking just a trifle quicker than usual, after having acknowledged the visual signal given by the trail boss. While making the pronouncement, he took noticeably more care to ensure he replaced his Stetson at the correct "jack-deuce" angle over his right eye. His tone and actions indicated how impressed he was by what they were about to do. Despite having accompanied Stone Hart on all the conventional trail drives made by the Wedge, his outward appearance of being at ease notwithstanding, he was as eager as the man he addressed to learn whether their latest endeavor was possible. "Let's go get her done."

"I thought you were *never* going to ask!" Geoffrey Crayne replied, trying to sound as nonchalant as he assumed the Texan to be and almost, but not quite, succeeding. "Oh well, I suppose it had to come sometime!"

"My ole pappy allus told me that 'most everything does, if you wait long enough," the *segundo* asserted, nudging the ribs of his blue roan gelding gently with the Kelly spurs on his boots. "Now just you take it slow and easy, you fool crowbait. Those critters down there aren't no Texas longhorns's've been raised to have right and proper respect for hossflesh. If you go crowding them, you're like' to get one of their sharp lil horns rammed up your favorite butt."

"Which I don't think would be a good thing to happen," the Bostonian breathed, having unknowingly duplicated the sentiments of Walter Johnson over how much more dangerous buffalo appeared in the wild. "Not unless you're a liber-radical soft-shell who reckons having things stuck up your butt is a perfect way to spend an evening."

While making the statement, striving to keep his emotions and mount equally in check, finding it easier to do so where the latter was concerned, Crayne accompanied Waggles from their place of concealment. Gazing beyond the still-unsuspecting buffalo, he watched Johnny Raybold and an Easterner appearing in just as leisurely seeming fashion almost opposite their position. Continuing his observation as he rode forward with the *segundo,* he saw other parts of riders leaving hiding places at intervals spreading westward on both sides of the herd. All were coming into view without haste, ready to take whatever kind of action their trail boss had warned might be required. From what they had been told, in all probability this would not be the same as would apply if they were dealing with even freshly caught *ladinos* and they had all received suggestions for how best to respond in the different circumstances.

To the uninitiated observer, the massive creatures grazing peacefully in the valley gave the impression of being a single herd under the control of one leader. Discussing their habits with the Ysabel Kid in Mulrooney, Stone and Waggles had concluded these could be helpful to the proposed transfer. The structure of such a gathering was much the same as would be the case with the only semidomesticated and free-ranging longhorn cattle that the Wedge crew were accustomed to handling. There was, however, a major and most vital difference to be taken into account. Buffalo were completely wild animals and lacked the inborn memories of association with man that even the wildest *ladino* never entirely lost or overcame. Regardless of this, the trail boss and his *segundo* had decided the very nature of their way of life could make them susceptible to persuasion.

As was the case with most subspecies of the family *Bovidae*—which included domesticated cattle and their wild progenitors—buffalo were gregarious by nature. Under the impulse of instincts generations old, whether traveling or pausing to take advantage of good grazing in a locality, they always preferred to remain in close proximity to one another. The majority of every herd was comprised of mature bulls, each with whatever cows he had been able to acquire and the immature offspring he had sired by them. Also present, driven from their respective families on approaching sexual maturity, were numerous younger males. Having as yet failed to gather females of their own—in fact some never would—they continued to mingle with the herd in "bache-

lor" parties. While the largest and strongest bulls tended to
take the lead on the move, there was no single leader as
such. Instead, if a dominant male should decide to move
away with his family, others would follow until the whole
gathering joined the exodus.

This was the particular pattern of behavior upon which
Stone Hart was gambling!

Such had been the care taken by the various pairs of men
that all had succeeded in reaching their positions and had
taken cover without being detected. While awaiting the signal to commence, they had been treated to the sight of the
buffalo's normal activities going on undisturbed. Calves not
yet fully weaned bleated and fed at the udders of their
mothers. Slightly older youngsters gamboled in their play
like oversize lambs, darting back to their family groups if
alarmed or if they had roused the wrath of an elder. Immature males staged mock fights that did much to establish the
position each would hold in the hierarchy of the herd. If one
of them should approach the harem of a dominant bull, a
more serious confrontation could take place. However, as
the mating season was over, these would not go beyond the
issuing of threats, which brought about the retirement of the
interloper. When not dealing with such a situation, the family leaders grazed peacefully yet with never-ending vigilance.

Unlike the majority of animals living habitually in fairly
open country, which tended to produce more reliance upon
vision than nostrils and ears to give warning of possible danger, the eyesight of buffalo was not exceptionally keen. Instead, despite close association with others of its kind and
the noises they invariably created, the main reliance for locating threats in the vicinity was placed on scent and hearing.

Catching the scent of human beings and horses, carried to
them by the light breeze, the nearest buffalo stopped their

various activities and looked in the appropriate direction.
On being able to make out the moving shapes slowly approaching, the family bulls in particular studied them warily.
Some of the big males adopted postures of threat, but these
were merely intended as a bluff. Seeing the menacing behavior was failing to produce the desired effect, bull after bull
elected to exercise discretion and move away. Those that
turned in any other direction except east discovered others
were swinging toward them. Accepting this behavior was
caused by a potential danger, they changed their minds.
Soon, every family and "bachelor" party was plodding along
as required by the men responsible for the departure.

"Well, we've got them on the move," Stone Hart drawled,
but his seemingly laconic tone did not fool the New Englander advancing slowly by his side. "Now all we have to do
is keep them headed toward their new home in Texas."

13

IS-A-MAN

Lying on a bed made from bearskin, in the darkness of the *tipi* placed at her disposal, Annie "Is-A-Man" Singing Bear was deeply perturbed. Never before, even though only her father was of the *Nemenuh,* had she been made to feel so ill at ease and unwanted in a Comanche village. However, she was shrewd enough to realize her lack of acceptance had not arisen because the community she was visiting was unique.

Nowhere else throughout the vast domain once claimed and roamed at will by the various bands of their nation—having driven or wiped out its former, less aggressive occupants in a fashion that a later generation would attribute solely to white men—could such a practically unchanged and traditional Comanche village be found. As far as living accommodation went, particularly in communities established upon reservations under the control of dedicated Indian agents willing to deal fairly with and look after the welfare of their charges (although there were some who used such a position of trust to line their pockets), there was an ever-growing tendency among the *Nemenuh* to adopt permanent residences after the style of the white people's dwellings.

Here in the depths of the Palo Duro country, although some were unoccupied and available perhaps a mile and a half away, there was no sign of the adobe or wooden buildings that were becoming an increasingly familiar addition to the landscape on the reservations. Instead, as had been the case for generations, the families were housed in *tipis*. Constructed of buffalo hides that were sewn together and stretched, flesh side out, over a conical framework of long, straight, and slender poles—pine or cedar being the woods most favored—that were peeled, seasoned, and pared down to a suitable diameter, these made easily transportable homes for people following a nomadic existence. Not only was such a structure weatherproof, being warm in winter and cool in summer, it could be erected in around fifteen minutes and, should there be a need to vacate a location hurriedly, could be struck for moving even more quickly.

In addition to the dwellings, the majority of the camp's occupants retained the traditional style of their nation, although a few of the men wore odd items of white manufacture. However, where buckskin would generally have been employed, the majority of their garments were fashioned from the hides of pronghorns. It was for this reason the *Kweharehnuh*—also known as the *Kwahihekehnuh*, "Sunshades on Their Backs"—band had become known to white men, against whom at a time not too long past they had frequently been in conflict, as the "Antelope" Comanche. Even before circumstances had restricted them to their present and much reduced territory, pronghorn had always been more readily available throughout what they had considered their personal "stamping ground" than the whitetail deer that provided "buckskin"—although does were more frequently used than bucks—for the other bands. Therefore, they had selected this animal as more easily obtainable for making clothes. However, while less dependent upon the huge beasts than most *Nemenuh* and other of the "Plains Indian" nations, they employed the hides of buffalo to supply walls for *tipis,* soles of moccasins, the outer covering for shields, and anything else that required toughness in use.

All the traditional weapons of the Comanche were still much in evidence around the village, looking much as they had for centuries except for metal having replaced bone or stone for the effective portions in some cases. However, in spite of the disinclination to adopt the dwellings and attire of the white man, this did not preclude a willingness to accept his firearms. The majority of these were Henry and Winchester repeaters. What was more, the latter included a few Model of 1873's as well as their predecessor, the Model of 1866. Regardless of how conservative he might elect to remain in other directions and no matter to which nation a brave belonged, nothing was more sought after and highly prized than one of those wonderful multiple-shooting products of paleface ingenuity. Nevertheless, the possession of so many repeaters in a single village—a misconception that would be created by fiction writers of a future generation notwithstanding—was very much the exception rather than the rule. Generally, they were only found in the hands of a very fortunate minority of any nation's fighting men.

Being conversant with the fairly recent history of the *Kweharehnuh* band, Annie was aware of how so many repeaters had come into their hands that even some of the *tuivitsi* as well as every *tehnap* were armed in this fashion. However, she knew the reason had nothing to do with the less than cordial treatment she was now being accorded on this, her second, visit to the village. Nor had the way in which she dressed, spoke, and behaved created the atmosphere.

Despite the tendency toward male domination, with women generally expected to accept less than equal status, these would normally have been considered approvable in such a conservative and traditionally minded community.

Just past her twentieth year, Annie was not more than five feet four in height. Although the *Pahuraix*—Water Horse—band of her father tended to be taller and more slender than the rest of the *Nemenuh,* she had come by the stocky build typical of most Comanches from her white mother. Her coppery-bronze attractive features, with somewhat slanted brown eyes and a snub rather than aquiline nose, were indications of her mixed birthright. Reddish brown, also a maternal trait, her hair dangled in two braids from beneath a plain dark blue cloth headband after the fashion of a warrior. However, the way in which the sleeveless and V-necked buckskin shirt and trousers conformed to the firmly fleshed, curvaceous contours of her torso and hips displayed in no uncertain manner that what lay beneath was *not* of the masculine gender. Nor was the rest of the attire she had brought with her, even the moccasins, feminine in style.

The invasion of what was generally considered masculine domain was not restricted to Annie's clothing. Within easy reach of her right hand was a weapon belt decorated with Comanche "medicine" symbols different from those of the *Kweharehnuh.* It carried a Colt 1860 Army Model revolver, the barrel and ramrod reduced in length to four inches, in an open-topped high-cavalry-twist holster on the right side. At the left, in a sheath made from the hide of a *wapiti*—erroneously called "elk" by Europeans—hung a J. Russell & Company "Green River" hunting knife with an eight-inch clip-point blade. Nor was this her sole armament. To her left lay a Winchester Model of 1866 carbine, its woodwork embellished by patterns made from brass thumbtacks, removed from its buckskin pouch inscribed in the same manner as her belt and serving to announce her membership of a *Pahuraix* war lodge. With them were an unstrung war bow and quiver of arrows, their flights protected from damage or the elements by a waterproof tarpaulin hood.

It was neither the masculine clothes nor the weapons that had caused the lack of cordiality. In fact, knowing why the former was worn and the latter carried, no Comanche living so close to the traditional way of their nation would have held either against a visitor of "Is-A-Man's" social status.

As was generally the case, despite her mother being white, Annie had been accepted as full Comanche by the *Pahuraix* band with whom she had spent all her life. From early childhood, she had always displayed greater proclivity toward masculine than feminine activities. Believing such a deviation from normal behavior was ordained by *Ka-Dih*, the Great Spirit, she was encouraged to adopt the life-style of a man. Receiving the same education as would any *tuinep* approaching adolescence, she had acquired all the skills needed to take her through being a *tuivitsi* and had attained the honored state of *tehnap*.

Before Annie could gain the desired advancement by riding on a war trail, or successfully "raiding"—as the *Nemenuh* called their favorite sport of stealing horses from people outside their nation—the *Pahuraix* had signed a peace treaty and accompanied the other bands, with the exception of the *Kweharehnuh*, onto reservations. Nevertheless, an opportunity to gain acclaim had arisen. Four Mexicans, *bandidos* masquerading as *vaqueros*, had come across and raped three girls from her village while drunk on tequila. Knowing there could be serious repercussions should vengeance be sought by the braves, she had claimed a *puha* dream forecasting bad luck would result if anybody other than herself tried to deal with the matter. Receiving support from the senior "old man" chiefs and medicine man, who shared her summations and desire to avoid trouble with the authorities, she had been granted seven days to carry out the mission. Before the time had elapsed, she had achieved her purpose. Catching up with the errant quartet, she had killed three. Her treatment of the fourth, which he claimed later—although not to any peace officer—was inflicted by twelve male braves, had rendered him completely incapable of ever again repeating the transgression.

Partly because of lack of evidence, a Grand Jury convened to investigate the incident at the request of the agent for the reservation who had accepted the Sun Oath of the elders, that no *man* of the *Pahuraix* had struck down the Mexicans, without pressing the matter further. Being Texans, wanting to retain peaceful relations with the Comanche, and having a repugnance for rapists, the jurors had publicly exonerated the band of being implicated in the matter. While Annie's participation was not revealed to white people in general, and those who suspected it kept silent, the story was passed around the other bands and even the *Kweharehnuh* received it. Furthermore, her handling of the affair had gained her acceptance as a *tehnap* and the granting of a "man-name" as befitting a warrior who had performed such a difficult and dangerous deed. From then on, among the *Nemenuh*, she was known as "Is-A-Man."

Even before her elevation to *tehnap*, finding Annie was intelligent and quick to adopt to changed circumstances as well as being appreciative of the need to live on amicable terms with white people, the agent for the reservation had trained her to be a most useful liaison between the two races of her bloodline. Given the added status, she had been able to carry out the task even more adequately. Nor were her activities along such lines confined to the *Pahuraix* and other Comanche signatories of the peace treaty. Once before, she had come to the Palo Duro country and helped avert trouble between the *Kweharehnuh* and the nearest white community. The leaders of the band had proved most grateful for what she had helped to do. Not only had she been treated as a honored guest, but she was told she would always be welcome at the village.

Annie's return was not for social reasons. It had come about as a result of disturbing rumors and reports received by the agent of the *Pahuraix* reservation. Usually there would not have been any need for her to engage upon such an investigation. Morton Lewis, a rancher in the vicinity, had a similar mixed birthright to her own. As grandson of Chief Wolf Runner, he had always had unrestricted access to the *Kweharehnuh*'s territory. Unfortunately, while in Kansas with a trail herd, he had broken both legs in a riding accident and could not return quickly enough to look into the matter that was troubling various white authorities.

Arriving on a three-horse relay used to speed the journey, Is-A-Man had found she was received less cordially than during the previous visit. She had not been turned away and, in fact, had been given accommodation in an unoccupied *tipi*. However, in spite of being told nothing to confirm her suppositions, what she had seen and deduced suggested there was a sound foundation for the misgivings of the agent and council of old-men chiefs for all the bands on the reservations.

Not only were a number of strangers present, men from several tribes not usually considered friendly by the *Nemenuh,* but there was a significant change in the leadership of the *Kweharehnuh*. In addition to others who would have received Annie in friendship, Wolf Runner, *Cicatriz Honorable*—Noble Scar—and the medicine man, Healing Hands, were dead. When she had sought to learn how they had met their end, even their families had been uncommunicative. Also conspicuous by his absence had been the senior old man chief, Ten Bears. However, despite meeting a similar reticence with regard to him, she knew something of his fate. He had left the village and, evading pursuers sent to prevent him, arrived at Fort Sorrel with an offer to make a treaty and bring his people peacefully onto a reservation.

The previous hierarchy had been replaced by men whom Annie knew to be hostile to white people and vociferous advocates of a return to the good old days of practically unrestricted roaming and riding the war trail. There was also a new medicine man. Much younger than was usual for one to attain a position of such importance, going by what she had heard, Prophet—as his name could best be translated into English—possessed powers exceeding those of his predecessor. She had also learned he claimed to be a hitherto unheard of son of the late *Pohawe*. However, because of the way death had come to those who offended or opposed *Pohawe* in the days of her malignant influence over the band, she had been considered more witch than medicine woman while she lived.

There had been much about Prophet that aroused Annie's curiosity and speculations. His build was typical of the *Nemenuh*, but his features suggested mixed blood. This could be expected, however, as *Pohawe* had had a Mexican mother. Instead of spending his time among the villagers, he was most frequently in attendance with the strangers and particularly those whom she found especially interesting. While they had the appearance and dressed in a style appropriate for warriors of Apache, Sioux, Cheyenne, and other "Plains" tribes, they always struck her—as did the medicine man—as not being entirely comfortable in such attire. What was more, they seemed equally ill at ease when squatting around a fire and eating in the primitive fashion of their hosts. Although they avoided coming into contact with her, their behavior reminded her of Indians she had met who had attended schools and acquired a taste for the ways of the white men, then were compelled for some reason to return to their own people.

Possessing a shrewd discernment, Annie guessed the change in her reception was at the instigation of Prophet. The story of how she had dealt with the Mexicans had reached the *Kweharehnuh,* losing nothing in the telling, so the rest of the population—even the new leaders—had been cordial at first. However, even though she had tried to avoid allowing her interest in whatever might be going on to become too apparent, the friendliness had changed to reticence and evasion. She had been too wise to delve deeper under the circumstances, guessing any attempt to do so would lead to her being asked, at the very least, to leave the village.

Despite being engrossed in trying to decide how she might gain the information she required, Is-A-Man was subconsciously on the alert for possible danger. Hearing a slight noise from just outside the *tipi,* then becoming aware of a surreptitious movement, she recognized it for what it was and reached for and slid the Army Colt from the holster with her thumb curled around the spur of the hammer and her right forefinger entering the trigger guard. Normally visitors paying a call during the hours of darkness announced their arrival openly and, when invited, came through the flap of the door. They did not, as whoever had disturbed her thoughts was doing, ease up the side wall and slip under it to gain admittance.

"Don't shoot!" a feminine voice whispered urgently, in response to the clicking as the hammer of the revolver was brought to fully cocked. "One keeps watch on the door and I had to come in this way!"

"Who are you?" Annie asked, just as quietly.

"I am Cooks Well," the visitor introduced, coming closer but halting beyond reaching distance to demonstrate she had no evil intentions. *"Pairaivo* of *Cicatriz Honorable* until he and the other leaders were poisoned by Prophet."

"You say Healing Hands was *poisoned*?" Annie queried, rendering the Colt safe without returning it to the holster. The question was provoked by her being aware that every experienced medicine man and woman had considerable knowledge of noxious potions and how they might be detected. "Doing it would not be easy!"

"I know, but Prophet has great *puha,*" the woman replied. "Not even Healing Hands could say how he made a boy sleep and feel no pain while pulling out a barbed arrow buried in his leg just by putting a medicine cloth over his face."

"I've heard he did that," Is-A-Man admitted. She did not say that, as a result of what she had deduced about Prophet and his associates, she had drawn a conclusion regarding how the feat was performed. "Why have you come, sister?"

"To tell you what you want to know," Cooks Well answered.

"And what is that?" Annie inquired, remembering she had seen the woman apparently on good terms with some of Prophet's adherents and wary of being tricked into admitting the true purpose of her visit.

"What has brought that misbegotten spawn of *Pohawe,* the witch woman, to our village," Cooks Well explained, and there was an anger and bitterness in her voice that Is-A-Man felt sure could not be simulated. "He claims *Ka-Dih* has ordained in a *puha* vision that every tribe must forget their enmity for one another, rise as one people, and drive the hated white-eyes forever from this land."

"Many have said that in the past," Annie pointed out,

making an effort to restrain her interest. "But nothing has come of it."

"He says it will this time," the visitor stated. "And tonight he will give a sign to those whom he has gathered here to prove his *puha* and his words."

14

BUFFALO ARE COMING

Moving with the silence learned to facilitate the successful stalking of very wild animals or avoiding detection by human foes, Annie Singing Bear passed along the alley between two deserted buildings in what had once been known to white outlaws as the town called "Hell." However, on reaching the end, she halted instead of advancing into the street. Even though she was carrying the Winchester Model of 1866 carbine and wore her weapon belt, she knew that to advance would be most unwise. The significance of discovering a man was keeping watch upon the *tipi* provided for her accommodation had not escaped her. It implied her presence would not be considered acceptable by the group gathered in front of a covered wagon, its canopy inscribed with medicine symbols, from the box of which they were being addressed by Prophet.

Questioning her nocturnal visitor further, what Is-A-Man had learned about the new medicine man of the *Kwehareh-*

nuh had been suggestive and disquieting. He had come accompanied by two less-than-savory half-breeds once employed as "go-betweens" with the population of Hell and a trio of Indians belonging to tribes unknown to Cooks Well. No better informed on the subject, basing the assumption upon what she had seen of them, Annie had concluded they too had spent more time among white men than their own people. Before displaying his possession of *puha*, Prophet had ensured his welcome by donating four large boxes of ammunition for the repeaters to the village. With the former supply from the outlaw town ended, this had been a certain way of becoming accepted by the warriors who had been in danger of running out of bullets.

There had been little the *Kweharehnuh* woman could say about the demise of Healing Hands, except that he—like all the others—collapsed and died without any noticeable distress or suffering. In the case of *Cicatriz Honorable*, shortly before sinking to the ground, he had complained to his *pairaivo* about what he believed to have been an insect biting his neck. While preparing his body for burial, she had found the sensation could have been explained by the sharp little sliver of wood sticking into his skin. However, she had not believed so tiny a thing could have been responsible for the death of her husband. Prompted by Is-A-Man, she had admitted that Prophet was nearby when the "bite" occurred and was blowing upon a medicine flute he frequently played despite it giving no sound a human ear could catch.

Nothing Annie had heard lessened her resolve to go to the meeting that Cooks Well said Prophet was holding at Hell. Even before the death of *Pohawe* on the outskirts, various events had given the town a medicine significance, which made it an area to be avoided. However, promised they would be safe under his protection, several *Kweharehnuh* braves had accompanied the "foreign" visitors to hear the great message he had received from *Ka-Dih*.

The problem of leaving the *tipi* had been simplified by the watcher being one of the trio who arrived with Prophet. Slipping out under the wall, having been told by Cooks Well where he could be found, Annie had had none of the difficulty she would have faced if trying to take a *Kweharehnuh* warrior by surprise. Turning when she came up to tap him on the shoulder from behind, the front of his shirt was grabbed by strong fingers. His attempted outcry was stifled when a knee, powered with muscles strengthened by hours of riding, took him at the most vulnerable point of masculine anatomy. Crumpling to his knees, pain rendering his vocal cords inoperative, two interlocked hands lashed against the side of his jaw. Pitched sideways, he was unconscious before he landed on the ground. Then, dragged into the *tipi*, he was bound and gagged so efficiently he would neither be able to escape nor raise the alarm on his recovery.

Realizing her actions would arouse Prophet's suspicions, if nothing worse, Is-A-Man decided she would be advised to quit the area once she had satisfied her curiosity. Helped by Cooks Well, she had packed her belongings and made ready for departure. Already wary as a result of the change in her reception, she had her three horses picketed close to the *tipi*. To one with a Comanche's training in all matters equestrian there was no trouble saddling and loading them. Thanking Cooks Well, she had left the village and arrived in the vicinity of Hell without being challenged. Although concluding the medicine man was so confident of his control over the *Kweharehnuh* that he considered lookouts unnecessary, she had left her relay and archery equipment at a safe distance from her destination. Although her summations had proved correct, she did not regret having taken the precaution.

Much to her satisfaction, Annie found she was able to see

the meeting clearly from her point of vantage. The light of a half-moon was being augmented with illumination from bull's-eye lanterns held at strategic positions by four Indians of different tribes. These belonged, she realized, to the group that she suspected had not lived with their respective people for some time. All the rest were staring at Prophet with rapt attention and he was speaking in a sufficiently carrying tone for her to hear what was being said.

At first, the harangue followed the lines Is-A-Man expected. She had heard it many times from young men with the kind of educational background she believed the speaker and his cronies had received. Speaking in English, his comments being interpreted for the benefit of the visitors by his companions—one of the half-breeds supplying the service for the Comanches—he had declaimed at length about the wrongs done to Indians by white men. The grievances first covered the slaughtering of peaceful villages, with old men, women of all ages, children, and babies sought as eagerly as the warriors for death at the hands of the "soldier coats." Then he denounced, just as vehemently, how the various nations whose representatives were present were being driven from their tribal lands.

What Prophet refrained from mentioning—and Annie had noticed others like him were equally omissive when making similar speeches on the reservations—was that the deliberate slaughter of innocents had never been purely the prerogative of the "paleface," or the Mexican Army, engaged in punitive actions. Indians riding the war trail— which happened far more frequently than a later generation would be led to believe by similar ethnically biased propagandists—showed just as little discrimination for age and sex when raiding a ranch, *hacienda,* mission, small settlement, or wagon train. Nor did the medicine man make any reference to the fact that Comanche, Kiowa, Sioux, Cheyenne, and

Apache had all either driven off or in some cases extermi-
nated the less warlike previous occupants of the terrain from
which they were in turn being dislodged by superior might.

Instead of stating both sides of either issue, Prophet, as
Is-A-Man anticipated, turned his attention to the fate of the
buffalo. While she could not deny that hunting by white men
was making considerable inroads upon the once vast herds,
in spite of knowing the dependence that many Plains tribes
had developed toward the great shaggy beasts, she gave little
credence to the stories spread by his kind about the way all
Indians supposedly treated them. Regardless of suggestions
that only a sufficient number for immediate requirements
would be taken and no part of the carcasses wasted, she had
been told many times of great hunts where whole herds were
killed and only a few prime cuts of meat were taken from the
bodies. Her belief was that the only reason even more had
not been slaughtered before the coming of the "paleface"
had been that the braves lacked the means to kill vast numbers.

Annie's theory had to some extent been supported by the
actions of the *Kweharehnuh* in the Palo Duro country. Given
repeating rifles and a more than adequate supply of ammunition—as payment from the white outlaws for being allowed to visit and live unmolested in Hell—instead of displaying an inborn aptitude for natural conservation, which it
was claimed every Indian possessed, the braves had practically wiped out all the larger wild animals through their
domain. This and the cutting off of the supply, she suspected, had been major factors in the decision of the elders
to send Chief Ten Bears to Fort Sorrel with the offer of a
treaty to go onto a reservation.

According to Prophet, the Great Spirit was angered by the
white men's willful destruction of his bounty. However, he
had not intervened because he felt the various tribes de-

served to be taught a lesson for allowing age-old rivalries to prevent them from taking concerted action against the hated white invaders of their domain. However, in a *puha* vision, he had promised he would cause the buffalo to return if they would forget past differences and join together in a war that would drive the palefaces from their land.

"It was *your* Great Spirit said this, Comanche?" asked an Apache, less flamboyantly attired than the delegates from other tribes.

"It was ordained by *Ka-Dih,*" Prophet replied, noticing that the question—which he had hoped would not be put by anybody—and his reply had to be translated into the respective languages of the delegates.

"I have not heard that any of our medicine men have had such a vision," commented a Cheyenne resplendent in white eagle-feather bonnet, dyed horse-hair shirt and legging tassels, bear-claw necklaces, hawk-bone hair skewers, and every other important meeting accoutrement of his people.

"Nor have any of ours," went on a Kiowa who was just as finely dressed, and, through their interpreters, the rest of the visiting factions stated the same.

"If it is the wish of your Great Spirit," supplemented the senior delegate for the Ogalalla Sioux, "let him give *us* a sign!"

While listening to what was being said, Annie had been studying the scene before her. One thing in particular had drawn her attention. A building immediately beyond the wagon, which had been halted at an angle across the street and had its team removed, had some kind of white covering on its wall. Considering how clean and fresh this appeared, she concluded it could not have retained such a pristine state since the departure of the original owners. Deciding the embellishment had been done at the instigation of Prophet, she wondered what its purpose might be.

The question was answered almost as soon as it occurred to the girl!

"Look!" the young man on the wagon shouted dramatically and pointed. "Buffalo are coming!"

Suddenly, despite the increased darkness caused by covers being closed over the fronts of all the bull's-eye lanterns, a picture of a herd of the massive and shaggy-coated beasts appeared on the white wall of the building indicated by the speaker!

Yells of surprise, close to terror, arose from almost all the other Indians present!

Equally startled in her place of concealment, Annie was hard put to restrain a similar outcry. Since going onto the reservation with the rest of the Water Horse band, she had seen "tintype" photographs taken by white men. Despite recognizing the resemblance of the portrayal, albeit far larger than any picture brought to her attention, she could not imagine how the effect was being produced. One thing she knew for certain. No matter how it was done, the illustration was producing the desired response from the assembled warriors of all the nations.

Before Is-A-Man could ponder further upon the matter, her instincts as a warrior gave warning that she was not alone in the alley. Turning with her right hand flashing to the hilt of the Green River knife, although her generally exceptional keenness of hearing had detected nothing of his approach, she found herself confronted almost at touching distance by what was clearly a masculine and well-armed figure.

"Easy there, Annie-gal!" the newcomer whispered only just loud enough to be heard.

The words were spoken in English!

Despite the language employed, the tall and slender shape facing Is-A-Man had the long, braided hair and clothing of an Indian. In his left hand, he held an eight-foot-long, feather-decorated war lance. A Winchester Model of 1873 rifle—identifiable by its frame being darkened steel and not the brass of the Model of 1866—hung by some kind of extemporized sling from his right shoulder. Nor were these the full extent of his armament. About his lean waist was an undecorated black gun belt with a big revolver, holstered butt forward at the right, and a massive white-handled knife was sheathed on the left.

"Cuchilo?" Annie gasped, and it was a tribute to her self-control that she was able to hold down her voice to the level at which she had been addressed. Also refraining from launching the attack she had intended making with the knife she had almost drawn, she returned its blade to the sheath and went on just as quietly, "How di—"

"That Apache bastard's heard us!" the Ysabel Kid warned, seeing a brave was turning to look in the direction of the alley. Leaning the lance against the left-side building, he continued quickly, but no longer, "Can you sound like you've been knifed and killed?"

"I reckon so," Is-A-Man confirmed, continuing to use English that now held a tone of puzzlement, watching the brave attract the attention of the rest of the group and cause the bull's-eye lanterns to have their covers opened to throw out light.

"Then do it and go down like you have!" the Texan commanded.

Wondering what was meant by the request and command, the girl did not waste time by asking. Instead, giving a croaking gurgle suggestive of mortal agony, she crumbled and flopped to the ground without leaving the shelter of the alley. Going down, she drew her Army Colt and, cocking the hammer, concealed it beneath her body as she landed. Then, after giving a few spasmodic twitches such as she had seen done by the victim of a fatal thrust from a knife, she went limp and awaited developments.

Nor were these long delayed!

Flanked by two men carrying lanterns to supply extra illumination, some of the Indians started toward the mouth of the alley!

Using the sling as a pivot, the Kid rolled the Winchester from his shoulder and into a firing position with deft speed. Aligning the barrel and working the lever rapidly, he sent half a dozen bullets to kick up a line of dust spurts from the street in front of the advancing men. Although all had some form of weapon on their persons, none were armed with rifles as a sign of pacific intentions, so the shots brought them to a halt. With this achieved, the Texan took his left hand from the rifle. Gathering up his war lance, he stepped forward until it was in plain sight. He himself could also be seen, but only well enough to establish he had the appearance of being an Indian brave, without allowing the details of his attire to be discerned.

"Stop there!" the Texan warned in fluent Comanche, making a gesture with the weapons he held, which served as an explanation unmistakable to those who did not speak the language of his maternal forebears. "Prophet, if anybody comes closer, I'll start shooting and some of it will come *your* way!"

"Stay where you are, all of you!" the young man on the wagon commanded in English, and this was translated for his cronies. Waiting until sure he was being obeyed, there was a suggestion of relief in his voice as he too employed the language of the *Nemenuh* to inquire, "Who are you, brother?"

"I am one called 'Bad Temper,' a lance carrier of the *Pahuraix*," the Kid lied, hoping the snarling timbre he put into his voice would prevent his somewhat slower-spoken

Pehnane dialect from being noticed by the Comanches in the group. "Coming here to hear your words, I found a spy watching and killed her—*him!*"

"A *spy?*" Prophet queried, noticing the emphasis with which the change of gender had been made as he was intended to. "Is it Is-A—?"

"Name no names, medicine man!" the Texan interrupted savagely, continuing to develop the plan he had thought out to enable him to leave peacefully with the girl instead of having to fight their way clear.

"As you will, Bad Temper," Prophet assented, concluding the name given by the newcomer was descriptive of his nature and considering any brave who elected to carry that most prestigious weapon, the war lance, would not be likely to accept mildly having a desire ignored. "Come and join us."

"Not yet," the Kid refused bluntly. "First I must get rid of the body."

"I'll have somebody come and help you," the medicine man offered.

"No!" the Texan denied, in a manner that warned he would brook no argument. "Listen well, medicine man of the *Kweharehnuh.* The one who has died has many powerful ones behind her—*him*—so I intend to make sure *nobody* can say why she did not return."

"Are the lance carriers of the *Pahuraix* all so easily frightened by what others may think of their actions?" inquired a young *Kweharehnuh,* seeking to prove himself worthy of being considered a *tehnap.*

"Come and find out how easily I'm frightened," the Kid suggested truculently, bringing up the barrel of the Winchester with his right hand. "But ask a blessing from your medicine man first, *tuivitsi!*"

"Bad Temper is a honored guest," Prophet announced,

bringing the attention of the youngster his way. "And there is no reason for his courage to be questioned."

"As *you* wish," the *tuivitsi* assented, aware of how those who thwarted the wishes of the medicine man frequently met with sudden and inexplicable death.

"May I ask what you're going to do, Bad Temper?" Prophet requested.

"From what I found on the way here, this one brought everything with her from your village," the Texan explained, allowing the rifle to turn downward again. "So I'll take it all and bury her and it where they will never be found."

"Do as you will, Bad Temper," Prophet authorized, deciding he might acquire a useful ally—or, at least, in view of the concern over possible reprisals by the influential associates of Is-A-Man, one over whom he had something of a hold—by showing such compliance.

"I *always* do," the Kid claimed, in keeping with the character he had adopted. "But remember this well, medicine man of the *Kweharehnuh.* If anybody tries to follow me, whoever it is had better be ready to go to the Land of Good Hunting. Because that is where I will send him and those who did not stop him coming after me."

"Go in peace," Prophet answered, knowing the latter part of the threat was directed at him. "I will see that nobody follows you, now or later, and all will welcome you on your return."

"I wouldn't count on *that,* you son of a bitch!" the Kid said in English, satisfied his requirements would be respected, but he said it to himself.

15
IT WILL MEAN ALL-OUT BLOODY WAR

"There's nobody coming after us, *Cuchilo*," Annie Singing Bear declared, looking from where she was being carried over the shoulders of the Ysabel Kid back to where they had come from. "So, if you're so minded, you can set me down and I'll walk the rest of the way."

"You'll not get any argument from me on doing that," the Texan replied, also in English, albeit in a somewhat breathless fashion. "God damn it, Is-A-Man, why didn't you tell me's how you've grown so much heavier since I last saw you?"

"Not all that much, damn it!" the girl protested as she was being set down on her feet. "The trouble is, you *Pehnane* never did have no get up 'n' go."

"I did have," the Kid contradicted, straightening his back and flexing his shoulders. Gesturing with the lance in his right hand, he elaborated, "Only it got up and went when I started toting you away from Hell."

Requested to assist with the negotiations for a peace treaty with the *Kweharehnuh,* Dusty Fog and the other members of Ole Devil Hardin's floating outfit had gone to Fort Sorrel. Although the prophecy of "Buffalo are coming" had yet to be made by the new medicine man, they had been gravely concerned by what they heard about his earlier activities from Chief Ten Bears. Learning of Morton Lewis being indisposed, it had been decided the Kid should go and investigate the latest developments. Calling at the home of the disabled rancher, he had been given valuable assistance by the foreman. This had not ended merely with the replacement mounts for the three he had used to supplement his magnificent white stallion so that he could speed the journey from the Fort. He had also been loaned a suitable black wig and the appropriate attire, used by Lewis when paying an extended visit to Chief Wolf Runner, as a disguise, and he had added a war lance to give further credence to his pose as a Comanche warrior.

Having traversed the terrain of the *Kweharehnuh* twice while helping Dusty and Waco close down the outlaw town, the Kid had no difficulty in returning there. He had intended using it as a starting point from which to locate the village, but seeing that the wagon had been halted at an angle in the street, and that the wall of the building had tightly stretched white sheets fastened to it, he had begun to wonder why this was being done. Leaving his horses in concealment, he had been making his way toward the town on foot when he heard somebody heading in the same direction. Concluding from the relay in use being left at a distance that the rider had not been invited to join those already assembled at the town, he had gone to look over the animals. Recognizing the *Pahuraix* medicine boot for the Winchester Model of 1866 carbine, which Annie had removed and left across one of the saddles, he had known who owned them and had set off to join her.

When the presence of Is-A-Man and the Texan had been detected by the Apache, he had thought quickly and concocted an excuse to get them away. Having ensured he could not be seen from the street, he had leaned his rifle and lance against the wall of the building. Waiting until the girl rose and holstered her revolver, he had hoisted her across his shoulders in what would come to be known as the "fireman's lift." Leaving her to carry his Winchester and the brass tack-decorated carbine, he had gathered up the lance and set off in the direction from which they had come. In spite of his superb physical condition, he had been under considerable strain while walking with such a load on his back. Nevertheless, he had continued to bear it until satisfied there was no further need. He was satisfied that, hoping to win him over as a willing ally, Prophet would not have allowed anybody to follow him and, should a search be made when he failed to return, it would be too late to interfere with their departure.

"What do you reckon's going on, *Cuchilo*?" Annie inquired, as they set off carrying their own weapons. "I know Prophet and those other white-educated young bastards want to get a war going between all the tribes and the white folks, but I can't see how they figure on doing it the way they are. Hell, the way he was talking, and with that fancy picture he showed, he reckons to make his medicine by some buffalo showing up and, seeing's how there ain't none anywheres around, there's no way he can make good on it."

"Hot damn!" the Kid exclaimed, remembering certain events during the last visit he and his *amigos* had paid to Mulrooney, Kansas. "Unlikely's it seems, there's just a chance he *might*!"

"Could the Wedge do it, though?" Is-A-Man asked, after having been told of the interest shown by Walter Johnson in the possibility of buffalo being moved like a trail herd of longhorn cattle.

"If anybody can, it's them," the Texan declared. "Only, knowing Injuns, they wouldn't bring buffalo anywheres near the Palo Duro country."

"Was that Johnson jasper even part Indian?" Annie inquired.

"Neither him, nor the two knob-heads he had with him," the Kid replied. "But they looked and talked like the kind of liber-radical soft-shells's are allus ready to lick the butts of anybod— Well, I'll be damned!"

"I never thought you *wouldn't*," Annie asserted, despite realizing the last words had been provoked by something her companion considered important. "But what's brought you around to figuring on it?"

"Four jaspers tried to gun down Dusty 'n' me last time we was in Mulrooney," the Texan explained. "We never found out much about them, but what we did made us think they was what folks in Europe call 'Bohemians' and, as they get took on regular as hired guns over there, 'd been sent by some folk's we'd got all riled up at us. Now I'm starting to wonder if they was Indians, not 'Bohemians,' and in cahoots with Johnson?"

"They could've been," Is-A-Man estimated. "But, even if they was, like you said, the Wedge have too much Injun-savvy to bring buffalo down this way."

"I've got a sneaking notion's Wedge wasn't hired to bring 'em all the way," the Kid answered, other memories arising now that he had started thinking about the visit. "They never let on's how it'd be buffalo instead of cattle they'd be handling. But after they'd sided Wedge again' some gandy dancers in a saloon brawl, Silent Churchman said some dudes was real nice fellers and the boys didn't mind having them along to learn about trail herding."

"That don't sound like soft-shells to me," Annie objected. "Ones's I've met've all been bumptious bastards's made you know they figured's how they was doing you a favor even knowing you was alive."

"Those two with Johnson were that kind," the Texan admitted. "But the others I met with the Wedge boys around town weren't. Fact being, going by what they said, they wasn't soft-shells at all 'n' didn't cotton to 'em."

"Then they wouldn't be mixed up with anything like we're thinking on," Is-A-Man stated rather than asked.

"Not if they knowed what they was doing," the Kid assessed. "Only that Johnson *hombre* was a real smooth-talking son of a bitch. He allus put me in mind of the kind of medicine showman's sells gold bricks made from painted lead on the side. Which being, he could've slickered Stone Hart and them into doing what's needed."

"Then we can't take a chance that it's not his game!" Annie stated grimly. "If it is and them buffalo're brought to where Prophet can show 'em off to the braves's he's got together, it'll mean his medicine's been made and proved 'n' there'll be all-out bloody war 'twixt Indians 'n' white folks from Texas to California."

"That's how I read the sign too," the Texan said somberly. "Dusty, Mark, Waco, 'n' Doc Leroy're waiting for me out a ways. The sooner we get there and tell 'em what we figure, the happier I'll be."

* * *

"Here are the night herders," Francis Morrell announced with malicious satisfaction, indicating the limp figures hanging facedown across the saddles of the four horses he and Kevin Roddy were leading. "The half-bree—*we* thought it better that all the bodies were together if they should be found before the uprising starts."

"Why have you covered them up?" the other young Easterner inquired, glancing at the motionless shapes covered in blankets, all lying around the campfire apparently using saddles for pillows.

"For the same reason I told the half-breed to have you bring in those four," Walter Johnson replied. "I hope those half-breeds coming to join Javelina can handle the herd well enough to get it to where it's needed."

"He assures me they're all experienced at handling cattle," Roddy claimed, his tone resentful as it always became when there was a suggestion of criticism to arrangements in which he was involved. "And, after all, we've got them this far without difficulty."

"First the Wedge and then these young men you've had me poison got them this far," the New Englander corrected. "And, if I'd had my way, they'd have been taken even closer. Now I can only hope your crowd are able to do the rest."

Although the task of transferring the buffalo had been without precedent, according to what Stone Hart had told Johnson before they parted, the task had presented far less difficulty than he had envisaged. In fact, he had asserted the journey was less eventful than more than one conventional trail drive in which he had participated.

Once the technique for persuading the herd to travel in the required direction had proved successful, the experienced Wedge trail crew had continued to do so. Employing similar tactics to those of the first day, each morning the mass of wild animals would be encouraged to set off from their overnight bed ground. By having the "point" riders move closer on one side and edge away at the other, the leaders were guided where it was necessary for them to go. Any individual buffalo, or group, that attempted to break away would be confronted by the nearest members of the crew. In every case, without needing to be approached too closely, caution and natural instincts had produced a return to the main body.

As time had passed, the animals had grown accustomed to their human escort. While this did not extend to allowing the men to actually ride among them, the Texans and Easterners had eventually been able to approach almost as near as would have been possible if dealing with *ladinos*. In its turn, this had permitted a greater amount of control to be exercised, a most important factor on those occasions when a river had to be crossed. Before long, the Texans were admitting their present charges were easier to handle than the usual herds put in their care. Not only were the buffalo able to cover as many miles in a day, but they proved less likely to take fright and stampede, as was all too frequently the case with longhorns.

Not only had Stone Hart guided the buffalo as requested by Johnson, contriving to avoid all contact with other human beings along the way, but he and his crew had been just as successful in teaching the willing young Easterners the necessary tricks of their trade. By the time that the herd had reached the border of New Mexico and Texas, Geoffrey Crayne and his companions had been judged competent to handle it unaided. Furthermore, acting upon what had amounted to an order from Johnson, Roddy and Morrell had each learned enough for them to be just passable as "night hawk"—relieving the Easterner trained as wrangler to watch over the *remuda* while he slept through the hours of darkness—as an alternative to their respective duties as cook's louse. In preparation for what lay ahead, claiming he was tired of the idle life of "businessman-turned-rancher," the New Englander had "volunteered" to spell his associates in the latter menial task. His real reason was that doing so would prevent suspicions being aroused when he would need to perform one part of the duties for the furtherance of the scheme.

Parting company with the Wedge at the junction of the

Canadian River and Rita Blanca Creek, the Easterners trained as trail hands had justified the faith in their ability expressed by Stone Hart. Not only had they carried out their respective tasks as taught by the Texans in a competent fashion, they had continued to follow such traditions as heckling the cook and ensuring that every man folded, secured, and placed his bedroll in the bedroll wagon before the commencement of each day's journey. Although they did not know exactly where they were heading, they had continued to keep the herd moving toward its destination.

Although Joseph Henry Abrahams had shown less than a warm welcome, Crayne and the other trail hands had not attached any significance to the apparently accidental arrival of a half-breed introducing himself as "Tom Javelina" just before they had broken camp that morning. When the crew had departed and the cook was occupied with his duties, he had told the conspirators that he had come from the Comanche now known to the *Kweharehnuh* as Prophet. Being informed that a sufficiently large party of men of mixed blood to handle the buffalo were not far behind, the hatred developed by Roddy and Morrell for the other young Easterners —aroused by having to accept menial positions instead of, as they expected, being considered leaders—had come to a head. In spite of Johnson saying he would prefer to leave the transfer of control until nearer the rendezvous, which was still at least twenty miles away where Prophet was waiting with the delegates from the tribes to "prove" he had "made his medicine," they had insisted it take place that night. Giving a reluctant concurrence, taking advantage of his self-appointed duties as cook's louse, the New Englander had been able to administer a potion brought from the East in the coffee he served to everybody in the camp except for himself and his fellow conspirators. Sending them to take care of the men riding night herd on the buffalo after the collapse of the others, having made a habit of delivering the beverage to those on duty, he had completed the task that he had assigned to himself by giving all the victims the appearance of being asleep.

"Let's put these four to bed like the others," Johnson suggested, waving a hand toward the horses.

"Would you two do it?" Roddy inquired, darting a glance redolent of nervousness at the figures draped across the saddles and turning away his eyes almost immediately. "I think I've eat something which didn't agree with me and my bowels are so upset I've got to relieve them."

"Mine are upset too!" Morrell claimed, and the New Englander noticed he was studiously avoiding looking at their victims. "I—I'll have to go right away!"

"That's all right, boys," Johnson said, his manner understanding. He concluded that the night herders had been hung over the saddles by the three men who had accompanied Javelina, but who had remained out of sight until they were needed to replace the victims. "When you've got that kind of problem, you can't hold it back without the danger of filling your pants, and none of us would want that."

While the younger men disappeared into the woodland on the fringe of which camp had been made for the night, the New Englander, showing a tenderness that they might have considered surprising under the circumstances, lowered each unmoving night herder to the ground. By the time Roddy and Morrell returned, he had laid and covered them in the same manner as their companions and the cook by the fire.

"You'd best put the horses with the *remuda,*" Johnson remarked, knowing this was being watched over by another of Javelina's companions.

"Of course," Roddy assented. "But first, I think this calls for a drink."

"So do I!" Morrell supported. "And I've a bottle of good brandy in my property that I brought ready for this."

"Well, Mr. Johnson," Roddy said, as his companion walked away. "Your part is over now. What do you intend to do next?"

"Go back east the shortest and quickest way I can," the New Englander replied. "Like you say, I've done my part and I'm not intending being anywhere west of the Mississippi River when the redskins rise."

"It wouldn't be advisable," Roddy admitted. "Not that Francis and I have anything to fear, of course."

"No," Johnson replied, his tone dry. *"You wouldn't be he —have."*

"Everything has gone off *splendidly*!" Roddy declared, trying to sound cheerfully enthusiastic despite a queasiness in his stomach that was not caused by something he had eaten disagreeing with him. It was created by the realization that he was now a party to wholesale and cold-blooded murder. Giving no sign to suggest that he had guessed the changed comment had been intended to be *"You wouldn't be here if you thought you had,"* he went on speaking so as to keep the conversation flowing. "Of course, I *never* doubted that it would. By the way, though. What really did happen at that hotel on the night you went to see 'Ivan Boski' and there was a fire?"

"What I've already told you happened," the New Englander replied, his manner warning he would not tolerate further questioning on the subject. Even though he would soon be quit of his associates and their evil scheme, he had no intention of leaving them in possession of facts that could incriminate him in arson and murder. "You just want to be thankful that everything turned out the way it did. I told you from the beginning that going after men like them could only end in disaster."

"It all turned out fine in the end," Roddy asserted sullenly, and was relieved to see his companion returning.

If Johnson had been watching Morrell, instead of having his attention held by the other young man, he might have had his suspicions aroused. Having collected three tin cups from the lowered tailgate of the chuck wagon, Morrell had gone to where his bedroll lay underneath the other vehicle. Opening it, he extricated two bottles from among the blankets. Having checked their labels carefully, he poured some of the contents from one into two of the cups. However, looking around to ensure he was not being observed by the New Englander, he used the other for the third. Concealing the second bottle and leaving the first in plain view, he returned to the fire. Handing the third cup to the New Englander, on it being accepted without the slightest hesitation he gave a quick nod while passing one of the others to his companion.

"To the buffalo!" Roddy toasted, lifting his cup in the traditional fashion.

"The buffalo!" Johnson responded and, despite his dislike for the two young men, drained the draught he was given to the last drop.

Noticing the eagerness with which his associates were watching him, the New Englander read something disturbing in their expressions. Even as he realized they were looking at him in a malicious and triumphant satisfaction, he felt a churning and nauseating sensation assailing him. Snarling an incoherent profanity, he reached for the revolver that—like all the other Easterners, including the pair before him—he had taken to carrying in a holster about his waist. Before he could draw it, his legs buckled and he collapsed onto his hands and knees.

16

SAVE MY BUFFALO

"I've been waiting for *this*!" Francis Morrell claimed, stepping forward to kick Walter Johnson in the ribs and topple him onto his back.

"You didn't think we ever intended to leave you alive, did you?" Kevin Roddy supplemented, walking around so he could drive his boot viciously against the body of the stricken New Englander whose reaction to the poison ingested while drinking the toast might have struck him and his companion as being very different from that of the previous victims. They too had collapsed, but without the convulsions wracking Johnson. "No lousy jailbait is going to have a chance to blackmail us when it's over."

"Now if that isn't just like a stinking Yankee soft-shell, or any other kind most likely," commented a coldly menacing masculine voice with a Texas accent. "Kicking and abusing a man when he's down, hurting bad, 'n' can't fight back."

"If he was stood 'n' could fight back," came a reply that,

while similar in timbre and accent, was feminine, "they wouldn't dare chance doing it!"

Spinning around, Roddy and Morrell stared as if unable to believe the evidence of their eyes. Although they had heard not so much as a sound to suggest somebody else was nearby, the speakers were walking side by side past the end of the chuck wagon.

Under different circumstances, any normal man would have found the sight of Annie Singing Bear well worth looking at. As an aid to avoiding unwanted interest during the hurried journey from the Palo Duro country, she had followed her usual procedure when traveling among white people. Her hair was concealed beneath a black Stetson with a Texas-style crown. However, the snugly fitting tartan shirt and old blue jeans that had replaced her Indian attire left no more doubts regarding her gender than had the clothing she wore on the night of Prophet's meeting in Hell. The weapon belt was about her midsection, but she was not carrying the Winchester carbine. Instead, she had the short war bow strung ready for use in her left hand, and a quiver holding several arrows was suspended across her back with the flights rising over her right shoulder.

Having no interest in women at any time, even when possessed of well-displayed curvaceous bodies, the two Easterners were even less interested at that moment. However, their interest in the male newcomer was not over whether he might be susceptible to their sexual inclinations. As he was clad in his usual all-black attire, they recognized the Ysabel Kid. Even if his words had not already done so, the expression on his Indian-dark face—which no longer had the slightest suggestion of innocence, babyish or otherwise— would have warned that his arrival at the night camp bode no good for them.

"H-how d-did y—?" Roddy croaked.

"Wh-why h-have you c-come?" Roddy supplemented in the same breath.

" 'Cause we've found out what you lousy soft-shell bastards're trying to do," the Kid replied. "So we've come to stop you!"

Which, although it did not answer the question asked by Roddy, was true enough!

When Dusty Fog had been told by the Kid what had taken place at Hell and the conclusions the Kid and Annie had formed, he had been able to confirm the most important part of the matter. Having met Waco after concluding the urgent private business that had caused his return to Texas, Doc Leroy had been at Fort Sorrel when the other members of the floating outfit arrived. Instead of going in search of his own outfit, he had accompanied them to the Palo Duro country. While he was able to confirm that the Wedge had been hired to drive a herd of buffalo, he had parted company with them long before their destination was made known to the rest of the crew. However, putting to use their considerable knowledge of trail driving, the small Texan and Mark Counter had calculated the most likely route for the buffalo to be brought to fulfill the "prophecy" made by the new medicine man of the *Kweharehnuh*.

Knowing Stone Hart would not participate in such an endeavor or even take the herd where it might be seen by hostile Indians, Dusty had deduced why the young Easterners had been brought in to handle the animals. Concluding that in the interests of maintaining secrecy the trail found by Colonel Charles Goodnight would be used, he had reasoned that a prominent geographical location would be chosen for the transfer of duties from Texans to Easterners, and he decided the junction of the Canadian River and Rita Blanca Creek was the most likely place.

Gambling upon his judgment, Dusty had set off with his

companions to verify it. Riding relay, they had made the best
time possible on the way. Calling at Amarillo to obtain fresh
mounts, they had had a fortunate meeting. Having gone
there after parting company with the herd, Stone Hart and
the Wedge were only too willing to reinforce the floating
outfit. Locating the buffalo and finding them being watched
over by night herders, Johnny Raybold had realized, just in
time to avoid letting his presence be known, that the herders
were strangers. Signaling for the Kid and Annie to join him,
using the call of a whippoorwill repeated in a prearranged
sequence, they had decided to reconnoiter the night camp
and find out was happening before taking any action against
the newcomers. This decision had been confirmed by Dusty
and Stone, the main body having been intercepted before
they were close enough for whoever was at the camp to hear
him.

Making their approach through the woodland on foot,
while Johnny went to check on something else, the first sight
of the camp had caused Is-A-Man and the Kid to wonder
whether the scout for the Wedge had been wrong with regard to the night herders. However, the peaceful appearance
that led to their doubts was proved to be false when they saw
the result of the toast drunk by the only three men still on
their feet.

"St-stop us?" Roddy croaked.

"Right here!" confirmed the Kid.

"Soames!" Morrell close to shrieked, gazing wildly into
the darkness, wishing that the policy of making camp sufficiently far from the buffalo to prevent them hearing any
commotion had not been followed that night. "Go and
ge—"

"If he's the feller's *was* riding night hawk on the *remuda*,"
the black-clad Texan drawled, having heard the call of a

whippoorwill from the direction in which the Easterner was looking, "he's been took good care of already."

"Kill them!" Roddy screeched as a realization of what had been said struck him and, with his companion duplicating the action, he grabbed for his holstered revolver.

It was a fatal mistake!

Although, like the other young Easterners, Roddy and Morrell had received instruction from the Texans since leaving Mulrooney and had practiced drawing their weapons, they had acquired only moderate proficiency. Which meant they were most ill-advised to make such an attempt to deal with Is-A-Man and the Ysabel Kid. Neither was exceptionally fast with a gun, as such things were judged west of the Mississippi River. However, Is-A-Man and the Kid did not attempt to meet the threat by using firearms.

Two knives were brought from sheaths and were sent through the air with a speed and precision that spoke of much experience. Thrown by a man who had been called *Cuchilo*—Knife—by the *Pehnane* Comanche as a tribute to his skill in wielding that particular weapon, the massive James Black bowie passed between two of Roddy's ribs and was long enough to slash through his heart. An instant later, directed with an equal accuracy albeit at a different portion of the human anatomy, the clip point of the J. Russell & Co. "Green River" blade buried into Morrell's throat to sever his jugular vein and windpipe. Neither Easterner had completed his draw. Nor were they able to. However, only Roddy made a sound, which was proof of how well Annie had reproduced it to help fool the Indians in Hell. Morrell was limited to a croaking gurgle as, twirling helplessly around with hands rising instinctively toward the hilt of the weapon taking his life, he and his companion sprawled to the ground.

"G-good work, si-sir—"

By the time that the first word was completed, Is-A-Man and the Kid had turned their right hands palm-outward to reach and wrap around the butts of their Colts. Even as they were starting to lift and twist the weapons from leather, they decided there was no need to do so. Face ashy-gray and haggard, Walter Johnson had forced himself into a kneeling posture. However, instead of trying to arm himself, he had his hands clasped against his stomach.

"Doc!" the Kid shouted, satisfied that the buffalo were too far away for the night herders to hear.

"Yo!" came the response distantly from beyond the woodland.

"T-too late for a doctor, I'm afraid," the New Englander assessed, easing himself until he was sitting in a huddled and clearly suffering manner. "I—I'm not much longer for this world and, what I'm sure my fate would be if I should live, that thought fails to distress me unduly. Are they both dead?"

"Close's they can be," the Kid confirmed, also glancing at the still-twitching bodies of the two young Easterners.

"You have my gratitude for that, sir," Johnson declared, a note of satisfaction underlying his hoarse voice. Then his face twisted into something close to a smile and he went on, "Although it's a pity they won't find out how I thwarted them."

"How'd you do that?" the Texan inquired, rolling Roddy over to retrieve and clean the blade of the bowie knife on his clothing.

"Th-those fine young men who brought the buffalo here after we parted from the Wedge," the New Englander answered, waving a hand weakly toward the fire. "Th-they're only drugged, not poisoned like I've been. I saw to that."

"Go take a look, Is-A-Man!" the Kid requested, deciding against waiting for the better-qualified assistant accompanying the party who could be heard hurrying through the woodland.

"Sure," Annie assented, turning from where she had completed wiping the blood from her reclaimed Green River knife on the shirt of her victim.

"You're wondering why those two didn't see through my subterfuge," Johnson asserted rather than inquired. "While willing to administer the poison, neither had the stomach for examining our victims. Nor, it seems, did any of the half-breeds in the advance party of those coming to take over the driving notice anything when loading the night herders they are replacing to be brought back here."

"Could be he's speaking true, *Cuchilo!*" the girl called, having raised a blanket and studied, then shaken vigorously by the shoulders, the unmoving man beneath it. "This feller's still breathing, but he's not waking up any."

"Nor will he for at least twelve hours," the New Englander claimed. "I intended to leave them weapons and sufficient ammunition to be able to reach safety on foot, albeit too late for them to prevent us from completing the delivery of the herd."

"Why'd you just drug 'em?" the Kid inquired, instead of pointing out the objections to the scheme that he—as a Westerner—could foresee.

"They were all fine, upstanding young men and I'd grown to like them, while finding the associates forced upon me growing increasingly obnoxious," Johnson explained, sensing the young Texan realized—as he himself had done when seeking some means of salving an unexpected growth of conscience—that there were dangerous disadvantages to what he had done. From what he had seen and been told about Javelina and the other half-breeds, they were not involved because of a desire to help the Indians, but for profit. It was unlikely that, even if they failed to discover the victims were not dead, they would have ignored the possibility of acquiring loot. Even if Johnson had prevented the theft of their clothing, the firearms were too valuable to have been left behind. Therefore, the Easterners would have recovered and been left far from any human habitation without weapons to defend themselves. On top of that, during the long hours they remained unconscious, they might have been attacked by predators or scavengers such as turkey vultures and coyotes seeking an easy meal. Nevertheless, he had consoled himself with the thought that, no matter what happened later, he had at least tried to ensure they survived. "Besides, although there was an excellent reason why I was compelled to help and give the appearance of seeking to ensure a successful outcome, I never really believed the scheme would work. After its failure, there was sure to be a most thorough investigation and, knowing how much influence their various families could bring to bear to find those responsible, I had no desire to spend the rest of my life under the constant threat of being hunted down and finally brought to justice."

"What's happened, Lon?" Doc Leroy asked, reaching the area illuminated by the campfire in the forefront of the Texans.

"Nothing you can deal with, regardless of the skill I hear you possess," the New Englander answered, before the Kid could speak. "At least, not for me. Even if an antidote exists for the poison I've been given, it's highly unlikely you would have any of it with you."

"Take a look at him, anyway, Doc," Stone Hart instructed.

"He's right," the slender and pallid-featured young Texan admitted, after having carried out an examination of the seated man. He spoke quietly to the trail boss and, because he took pride in his medical abilities, said a trifle sadly,

"There's nothing I can do for him. Fact being, he'll soon be gone."

"There's no need to whisper," Johnson said, without trying to rise from where Doc had eased him to lie on his back against a saddle for a pillow. "I know what my chances are and can only take comfort from knowing Roddy and Morrell have preceded me to Hell, as that is where I presume I will be going."

"Who else is behind what you were trying to do?" the trail boss asked. "Was it that damned Society you said you represent?"

"Not so far as I know, sir," the New Englander replied. "Although some of its members might have been involved, my impression is that the majority were no more than innocent dupes."

"You must know who hired you," Dusty Fog pointed out.

"I *don't* know, sir. The offer came through somebody I was not in a position to refuse," Johnson declared, then raised his right hand in a weak yet definitely prohibitive gesture. "Don't ask me from whom it came. Dying I may be, but I've *never* betrayed an associate and, although I suppose they deserve it for having forced me into this sorry affair, I won't break that rule. I will say one thing, though. When my young friends wake up, as I am now certain they will, tell them to spread the word of what happened to me around back east and I can promise you my associates will make the men behind Roddy and Morrell hard to find."

"We'll do that," Dusty promised and, sharing his unspoken assumption that it might be preferable not to have the affair made public, Stone nodded concurrence.

"Th-there's another thing," the New Englander went on, but he was clearly finding it difficult to speak. "I've grown fond of those big, shaggy, ugly creatures I caused to be brought so far from their natural habitat—"

"And?" the small Texan prompted.

"If you possibly can, gentlemen," Johnson requested, making a visible effort to do so, "save my buffalo from being killed!"

"We'll do the best we can for them!"

This time it was the trail boss of the Wedge who gave the assurance, and the *segundo* of the OD Connected signified agreement!

* * *

"Where're the dudes?" asked one of the ten men of obvious mixed birthright, gazing around as they rode into the light of the campfire.

"Maybe to collect wood," Tom Javelina replied, bringing his mount to a halt and starting to dismount.

"All three of 'em?" growled a third half-breed, no more prepossessing in appearance than the rest of the well-armed party.

"What I saw of 'em, neither of the two young'n's'd do a lick of work unless the other two was helping," Javelina explained, then he waved a hand toward the still and blanket-covered shapes around the fire. "Don't forget, everything you take from 'em goes into the pot so's the boys riding night herd and with the *remuda* get their fair share."

"Sure, Tom!" chorused the rest of the men, but their tones held little assurance that they were sincere.

Dismounting and leaving the horses ground-hitched by dangling reins, the half-breeds fanned out as they hurried to collect what they expected would be easily acquired loot. Moving faster than the rest, the man who had asked about the "dudes" arrived first. Bending over the nearest figure, he jerked off the blanket.

"Surprise!" Peaceful Gunn greeted, thrusting himself into a sitting position with a cocked Colt Peacemaker in each hand.

As was so often the case throughout his life, Dusty Fog had been successful in duplicating the thoughts of a man against whom he would be in contention. Knowing the camp was between the buffalo and—as a result of the four Indians who were to act as liaison between the various conspirators being killed in Mulrooney—the most likely direction from which the replacement trail crew would arrive, he had guessed they would call at the camp for a meal and to loot what they believed to be the corpses of their predecessors before going to the animals. Stone Hart had agreed they should base their strategy upon this supposition. Having been removed by the Ysabel Kid, Annie Singing Bear, and Johnny Raybold, the night herders had had their places filled by Texans. Hiding the bodies of Walter Johnson, Kevin Roddy, and Francis Morrell, the rest of the party had positioned themselves ready to deal with the contingency that Dusty had envisioned.

Spluttering an alarmed profanity, the first half-breed to have reached the supposed victims jerked erect. Seeing that more of the recumbent, concealed shapes were starting to sit up and also held weapons, he tried to bring out his revolver. Under the circumstances, the attempt was futile and doomed to failure. Appreciating the full extent of the devastation and loss of human lives that would have occurred throughout the West if the scheme had achieved its purpose, Peaceful had no compunction over dealing with such a reaction. His right-hand Colt barked and, entering beneath the man's chin, ranged onward through the brain to kill instantaneously. While the lifeless body of the would-be looter was toppling away from his intended victim, there was more shooting.

Not all the party seeking to prevent the delivery of the buffalo were posing as drugged Easterners around the fire. Is-A-Man, the trail boss, his *segundo,* and the members of the floating outfit had taken concealment in the bed and chuck wagons. Following advice given by Dusty, based upon considerable experience of such matters gained while serving as a peace officer, none of them were relying upon handguns. Seeing the rest of the newcomers were displaying hostility, their Winchesters—five rifles and two carbines— were more suitable than revolvers would have been over the distances involved.

Taken completely unawares, although far from cowards and usually well able to handle guns, the half-breeds were far from at their most efficient. To add further to their misfortunes, they were opposed by a girl trained as a Comanche warrior and by men who shared the revulsion felt by Peaceful Gunn for what they were planning to do. Only one of them succeeded in clearing leather. Even though he got his gun out, Tom Javelina was cut down by lead from the carbine in Annie's hands and the Kid's rifle before he could get off a shot. Three more of the half-breeds took lead, one being flung backward under the impact of eighteen .32-caliber buckshot balls from the sawed-off shotgun owned by Joseph Henry Abrahams, and which Silent Churchman had declared he would wish to be used in retaliation for what had happened to him. Although untouched by flying bullets, provoked by near misses, the rest of the would-be looters concluded discretion was the better part of valor. Dashing to the alarmed and rearing horses, they displayed riding skill of a high order by mounting the nearest animal, regardless of its behavior, and racing away.

"Take after them, Lon, Annie!" Dusty commanded, lowering his smoking Winchester Model of 1873 carbine and noticing with satisfaction that his companions were also refraining from firing at the fleeing men. "If they're only lighting a shuck, let them keep going."

"And if some of them're figuring on heading down to let

Prophet know what's come off here?" the Kid inquired, although he could guess the answer.

"In that case," the small Texan replied, his voice as cold and deadly as a judge announcing a sentence of death, "stop them in their tracks!"

17
NO BUFFALO ARE COMING

"Well, the Apaches have left," announced the interpreter for the Sioux, entering the *tipi* presented by the *Kweharehnuh* to their new medicine man and finding all his associates present. His tone was filled with a malicious mock commiseration, which the others knew indicated satisfaction over being able to deliver bad news affecting somebody else. "And, from what I've been told, the Cheyenne are thinking of going."

"Those Throat Cutters of yours were the first to start whining when the buffalo didn't show up," growled the young man who had translated for the Apache. "I'm surprised they haven't run away already!"

"They won't leave so long as they're getting their idle bellies filled with food," claimed the representative of the Cheyennes, having a very personal relationship that made him willing to back up the previous speaker.

"Don't start *bickering*, damn you!" Prophet commanded

savagely, his own nerves being equally on edge as a result of the animals, upon which the outcome of his venture depended, having failed to put in the appearance he had promised. "Javelina warned us that he couldn't garantee to have them show up on time, and they might be a day or two late."

"So you told us the second day after they were *supposed* to be here," the interpreter for the Kiowa reminded sourly. "And that was *four* days ago. I don't know about those other savages, but my crowd is getting harder to keep hanging around. Even your conjuring tricks and the magic lantern are beginning to pall."

As was always the case when the college-educated Indians gathered together, because none of them knew more than a limited number of words of any tribal language other than their own, they were speaking in English. They also considered it advisable to do so among themselves, particularly when discussing their reason for being at the *Kweharehnuh* village, as it prevented what they were saying from being understood by the people upon whom they were depending to put them in the positions of power they craved.

Looking from one to another of his associates, Prophet hoped he was showing less of the trepidation that was growing increasingly stronger among them with each passing day when they had to tell their delegations that the promised sign from *Ka-Dih* still had not been given. When Walter Johnson had met with Tom Javelina at a town near the junction of the Canadian River and Rita Blanca Creek, having gone there under the pretense of collecting supplies for a celebratory dinner on the night before parting company with the Wedge, he had reported the expected delivery date to the medicine man. Therefore, the prediction had been based upon the time he had quoted.

At first, the delegates and men of the village had accepted Prophet's explanation that bounty from the Great Spirit could not be hurried, and they all awaited the coming of the herd without complaint. However, with each succeeding day, they had shown less sign of being impressed by the spectacular conjuring tricks he had used to help him attain his position. Even the—to them—still inexplicable picture of the buffalo upon the white-covered wall of whichever building was selected in the town of Hell had lost its appeal, and he had been hard-pressed to prevent the growing disillusionment over the failure of his prophecy to be fulfilled.

"What're we going to do?" the Sioux demanded.

"Wait!" the medicine man replied, the question having been directed at him.

"For how much longer?" the Sioux snarled.

"Until I say otherwise," Prophet stated, pulling what appeared to be an Indian-made wooden flute from his left sleeve and toying with it. "Have you any objections?"

Although the Sioux scowled malevolently at the apparently innocuous action and laid his right hand upon the butt of the revolver that he—like all the others—carried tucked into the waistband of his trousers, there was an interruption before he could respond further to what had clearly been a challenge.

"Prophet, this is Bad Temper, lance carrier of the *Pahuraix*, calling for you to come out and make talk!"

"What's brought *him* back?" the medicine man asked and, not being averse to finding an excuse to avoid a confrontation with the Sioux, came to his feet.

"Who?" the Cheyenne inquired.

"That damned savage who killed the half-breed girl the first night we showed them the buffalo," Prophet replied. "Come on. Perhaps he's seen the real thing!"

Starting to leave the *tipi*, followed by his companions, Prophet came to a halt in the doorway and stared at the sight that met his gaze. A large number of villagers and delegates were gathered and more were coming from all sides, but he gave them no more than a cursory glance. His main attention was devoted to two men and a woman standing well in the forefront of the crowd. From all appearance, apart from the lance being absent and the Winchester being in a long, fringed buckskin pouch inscribed by medicine symbols, the taller was dressed and armed as he had been in the alley at Hell. The second man was a small Texas cowhand with dusty-blond hair. Despite the two white-handled Colts butt forward on a gun belt, he hardly appeared to be worthy of notice.

The same did not apply to the female member of the trio!

It was the half-breed girl who called herself "Is-A-Man"!

"Y-you said you'd killed her!" Prophet gasped, wrenching his gaze from Annie Singing Bear to the "Indian" with an effort of will.

"I lied," the Ysabel Kid confessed calmly. Then he raised his voice and, looking over his shoulder at the gathering crowd, made his *Pehnane* dialect even more pronounced as he continued in his maternal language. "Is this the great medicine man of the *Kweharehnuh,* a man who doesn't know a Wasp from a Water Horse?"

"What do you mean?" Prophet snarled.

"I'm not a *Pahuraix,* nor even a full-blood *Pehnane,* although there is no lie about this medicine pouch, and I am a member of the Dog Soldier war lodge," the Kid replied, bringing his gaze to the speaker and reaching with his left hand to remove the wig. "My man-name is *'Cuchilo,'* the Knife. Is-A-Man you know, and this one with me is Magic Hands, who broke the medicine of the Devil Gun—in other words, you stinking half-breed son of a bitch, he's Captain Dusty Fog!"

If the exclamations from the men behind him were any guide, Prophet decided they too had heard of Captain Dusty

Fog. What was more, like the Comanches, the Kiowa delegation in particular probably knew why the sobriquet "Magic Hands" was given. With it had also been conferred a status of blood brother, which made the small Texan—who somehow no longer gave the impression of lacking size—*persona grata* in the *Kweharehnuh* village.

"Why have you come back?" the medicine man asked, trying to avoid being shoved forward by his associates as they crowded from the *tipi* and, as the final part of the introduction had been made in that language, also speaking English.

"To say you lied when you spoke of *Ka-Dih* giving a sign for all the nations to join and make war on the white man," the Kid proclaimed in ringing tones, reverting to Comanche. Even without looking around, he could hear his words being translated into other languages without the need for the college-educated interpreters forming a line around the man he was addressing. Knowing Indians, it was as he had anticipated. Each delegation had included at least one brave conversant in the tongue of their hosts. "No buffalo are coming!"

"How do you know?" Prophet asked, instead of trying to quell the wave of excited comments that arose among the crowd.

"We've stopped them," the Kid replied.

"Javelina is dead and those of his bunch who lived ran off without any the one of 'em trying to come and warn you," Annie supplemented in English, sounding just a trifle disappointed there had been no attempt to deliver the news. Gesturing with the Winchester carbine she held before her in both hands, bared of its medicine boot, she went on, "That smoke down to Hell's coming from your wagon, along with all that fancy white man's conjuring gear 'n' magic lantern. Those jaspers you had minding it for you just somehow couldn't stop us setting fire to it."

"I must seek guidance on this," Prophet asserted, starting to raise the wooden tube he was still holding. "This medicine flute will let us see what the wishes of *Ka-Dih* are."

With that, confident his associates would realize his intentions and be ready to take the appropriate action, the medicine man inflated his lungs and brought the tube to his lips. Even as he was doing so, gloating inwardly over what he expected to happen, his proposed victim proved his intentions were known to more than just the Indians to either side of him. Flung with power and precision, the black wig flew to strike Prophet on the face. The unexpected attack caused him to inadvertently breathe in sharply instead of blowing through the tube. Before he could stop it, shock ripped through him as he felt the deadly sliver of wood he should have expelled at the Kid being sucked into his mouth. Although there was only a slight stabbing pain on his tongue, which instinctively sought to eject it, Prophet knew what this implied. Gasping in horror, he allowed the tube to fall from his hands and clasped them futilely—as he knew—to his face.

Ready for Prophet to send off a poison-tipped sliver of the kind that had played a major part in his rise to power among the *Kweharehnuh*, not even their previous medicine man having heard of such a device, the other college-educated Indians snatched at the guns in their respective waistbands as the wig was being thrown at him. Before any of them could extract his weapon, they discovered how Dusty had acquired the sobriquet used as part of the introduction by the Kid. Crossing so fast the human eye could barely follow their movements, his hands brought the bone-handled Colt Civilian Model Peacemakers from their well-designed holsters. Turning the barrels outward at waist level, half a second after the commencement of the movements, he fired them practically at the same instant. For all that, before either could clear his weapon, the interpreters for the Apache and the Sioux each received a .45-caliber bullet in the left breast.

Like the small Texan, Is-A-Man had been told by the Kid about the secret of the "flute" and its poisoned darts. Therefore, she too was prepared for trouble. Bringing around her carbine with the smoothly flowing rapidity of long practice, she also opened fire, guided by instinctive alignment. Working the lever as swiftly as possible, she spread five shots before her like the spokes of an invisible wheel. Hit by two, either of which would have been fatal, the translator for the Kiowa followed Dusty's victims as they reeled against and rebounded helplessly from the side of the *tipi* to sprawl dying on the ground.

As soon as the steps to prevent Prophet using the blow pipe had been taken, the Kid was shaking the medicine boot from his Winchester. While the right hand was turning the barrel, the left flashed over to close upon its wooden foregrip. Such was the deft speed he employed and the skill he had attained, the bullet he discharged found its intended mark by passing through the center of the Cheyenne speaker's forehead. Spinning around, the stricken man collided with Prophet and they fell together through the door of the *tipi*. Neither would walk out again.

"There is no need for weapons!" the senior chief of the *Kweharehnuh* declared, as the girl and the Texan swung toward the crowd ready to take whatever action might prove necessary. Indicating the bodies outside and two pairs of unmoving feet showing through the entrance to the *tipi*, he went on, "The medicine flute took Prophet's life this time, which means he had lost favor with *Ka-Dih* and that is why those others died with him. Let all who came here because of him leave in peace."

"We can put up our guns, Dusty," the Kid stated with
confidence. "It's safe to do it now and, seeing's how the
buffalo won't be coming, there isn't going to be any uprising
of all the tribes."

APPENDIX ONE

Following his enrollment in the Army of the Confederate States, by the time he reached the age of seventeen, Dustine Edward Marsden "Dusty" Fog had won promotion in the field to the rank of captain and was put in command of Company "C," Texas Light Cavalry. At the head of them throughout the campaign in Arkansas, he had earned the reputation for being an exceptional military raider and a worthy contemporary of John Singleton "the Gray Ghost" Mosby and Turner Ashby, the South's other leading exponents of what would later become known as "commando" raids. In addition to preventing a pair of pro-Union fanatics from starting an Indian uprising, which would have decimated much of Texas, and thwarting a Yankee plot to employ a variant of mustard gas in the conflict, he had supported Belle "the Rebel Spy" Boyd on two of her most dangerous assignments.

At the conclusion of the War Between the States, Dusty

became *segundo* of the great OD Connected ranch—its brand being a letter O to which was attached a D—in Rio Hondo County, Texas. Its owner and his maternal uncle, "Ole Devil" Hardin, C.S.A., had been crippled in a riding accident. This placed much responsibility, including the need to handle an important mission—with the future relationship between the United States and Mexico—upon his young shoulders. While doing so, he met Mark Counter and the Ysabel Kid, who did much to bring about a successful conclusion. After helping to gather horses to help replenish the ranch's depleted *remuda,* he was sent to assist Colonel Charles Goodnight on the trail drive to Fort Sumner, New Mexico, which would do much to help Texas recover from the impoverished conditions left by the War. With that achieved, he had been equally successful in helping Goodnight convince other ranchers it would be possible to drive large herds of longhorn cattle to the railroad in Kansas.

Having proven himself to be a first-class cowhand, Dusty went on to become acknowledged as a very competent trail boss, roundup captain, and town-taming lawman. Competing at the first Cochise County Fair in Arizona, against a number of well-known exponents of fast drawing and accurate shooting, he won the title "Fastest Gun In the West." In later years, following his marriage to Lady Winifred Amelia "Freddie Woods" Besgrove-Woodstole, he became a noted diplomat.

Dusty never found his lack of stature an impediment to his achievements. In fact, he occasionally found it helped him to achieve a purpose. To supplement his natural strength, also perhaps with a subconscious desire to distract attention from his small size, he had taught himself to be completely ambidextrous. Possessing perfectly attuned reflexes, he could draw either, or both, of his Colts—whether the 1860 Army Model or their improved "descendant," the fabled 1873

Model "Peacemaker"—with lightning speed and shoot most accurately. Furthermore, Ole Devil Hardin's "valet," Tommy Okasi, was Japanese and a trained *samurai* warrior. From him, as was the case with the General's "granddaughter," Elizabeth "Betty" Hardin, Dusty learned *jujitsu* and *karate*. Neither form of unarmed combat had received the publicity they would be given in later years and were little known in the Western Hemisphere at that time. Therefore, Dusty found the knowledge useful when he had to fight with bare hands against larger, heavier, and stronger men.

APPENDIX TWO

With his exceptional good looks and magnificent physical development, Mark Counter presented the kind of appearance that many people expected of Dusty Fog. It was a misconception that they took advantage of on occasion and once was almost the cause of the blond giant being subjected to a murder attempt although the small Texan was the intended victim.

While serving under the command of General Bushrod Sheldon during the War Between the States, Mark's merits as an efficient and courageous officer were overshadowed by his unconventional taste in uniforms. Always a dandy, coming from a wealthy family and, later, given independent means in the will of a maternal maiden aunt, had allowed him to indulge in his whims. His selection of a skirtless tunic, for example, had been much copied by the young bloods of the Confederate States' Army—including, although they had not yet met, Captain Dusty Fog—despite considerable opposition and disapproval on the part of hidebound senior officers. Following his return to civilian life, he became considered the arbiter of fashion among Texas' cowhands.

When peace came, Mark followed Sheldon into Mexico to fight for Emperor Maximilian. There, he met Dusty and the Ysabel Kid, helping the former to accomplish a very important mission. On returning to Texas, he had been invited to join the OD Connected ranch and become a founding member of its floating outfit. Knowing his father and two older brothers could run the great R Over C ranch in the Big Bend country without needing his aid—and suspecting life might prove more exciting in the company of his two *amigos*—he accepted.

An expert cowhand, Mark was soon known as Dusty's right bower. He had also gained acclaim by virtue of his enormous strength and ability in a roughhouse brawl. However, due to being so much in the company of the Rio Hondo gun wizard, his full potential as a gunfighter tended to be given less attention. Nevertheless, men who were competent to judge such matters stated he was second only to Dusty in speed and accuracy.

Many women found Mark's handsome appearance irresistible, including Miss Martha "Calamity Jane" Canary. Nevertheless, in his younger days, only the lady outlaw Belle Starr held his heart. It was not until several years after Belle's death that—we suspect due to matchmaking by Elizabeth "Betty" Raybold, née Hardin—he courted and married Dawn Sutherland, whom he had first met on the trail drive led by Colonel Charles Goodnight to Fort Sumner, New Mexico. The discovery of vast oil deposits on the ranch they bought added wealth to them and forms a major part of the income for the present-day members of the family. At least three descendants of Mark and Dawn, each of whom inherited his looks and physique, achieved fame on their own account.

Recent biographical details received from the current head of the family, Andrew Mark "Big Andy" Counter, establishes that Mark was descended on his mother's side from Sir Reginald Front de Boeuf, notorious as master of Troquilstone Castle in Medieval England and who lived up to the family motto, *Cave Adsum*. However, although a maternal aunt and her son, Jessica and Trudeau, gave signs of having done so, the blond giant had not inherited the very unsavory character and behavior of this ancestor.

APPENDIX THREE

Raven Head, only daughter of Chief Long Walker, war leader of the *Pehnane*—Wasp, Quick Stinger, Raider—Comanche's Dog Soldier lodge, and his French Creole *pairaivo*, married an Irish-Kentuckian adventurer, Sam Ysabel, but died giving birth to their first child. Baptized "Loncey Dalton Ysabel," the boy was raised after the fashion of the *Nemenuh*. With his father away so much of the time on the family's combined business of mustanging—catching and breaking wild horses—and smuggling, his education had largely been left in the hands of his maternal grandfather. From Long Walker, he learned all those things a Comanche warrior must know: how to ride the wildest freshly caught mustang, or make a trained animal subservient to his will when "raiding"—a polite name for the favorite pastime of the male *Nemenuh,* stealing horses—how to follow the faintest tracks and just as effectively conceal signs of his own passing; how to locate hidden enemies, or keep out of sight himself when the need arose; how to move in silence through the thickest cover and on the darkest nights; how to know the ways of wild creatures and, in some cases, imitate their calls so that others of their kind might be fooled.

The boy proved a most excellent pupil in all the subjects, especially where protecting himself was concerned. He had inherited his father's Kentuckian rifle-shooting skill and, while not *real* fast on the draw—taking slightly over a second to bring out and fire his weapon, whereas a top hand could practically halve that time—he performed passably with his Colt Second Model of 1848 Dragoon revolver. He won his *Pehnane* "man-name," *Cuchilo,* Spanish for Knife, by his exceptional skill in wielding one. It was claimed by those best qualified to judge that he could equal the alleged designer in performing with the massive and special type of blade that bore Colonel James Bowie's name.

Joining his father in smuggling expeditions along the Rio Grande, the boy became known to Mexicans of the border country as *Cabrito:* a name that arose out of hearing white men refer to him as the "Ysabel Kid," but was spoken *very* respectfully in that context. Smuggling was not an occupation to attract mild-mannered pacifists, yet even the roughest and toughest of the bloody border's brood had come to acknowledge it did not pay to rile up Big Sam Ysabel's son. The education received by the Kid had not been calculated to develop any overinflated belief in the sanctity of human life. When crossed, he dealt with the situation like a *Pehnane* Dog Soldier—to which war lodge of savage and most efficient warriors he had earned initiation —swiftly and in an effectively deadly manner.

During the War Between the States, the Kid and his father had commenced by riding as scouts for Colonel John Singleton "the Gray Ghost" Mosby. Later, their specialized knowledge and talents were converted to having them collect and deliver to the Confederate States' authorities in Texas supplies that had been purchased in Mexico or run through the blockade by the United States Navy into Matamoros. It was hard and dangerous work, but never more so than on the two occasions when they became involved in assignments with Belle "the Rebel Spy" Boyd.

Soon after the War ended, Sam Ysabel was murdered. While hunting for the killers, the Kid met Dusty Fog and Mark Counter. When the mission upon which they were engaged was brought to its successful conclusion, learning that the Kid no longer wished to go on either smuggling or mustanging, the small Texan had offered him employment at the OD Connected ranch. It had been in the capacity of scout rather than ordinary cowhand that he was required, and his talents in that field were frequently of the greatest use as a member of the floating outfit.

The acceptance of the job by the Kid had been of great benefit all around. The ranch obtained the services of an extremely capable and efficient fighting man. Dusty acquired another loyal friend who was ready to stick by him through any kind of peril. For his part, the Kid was turned from a life of petty crime—with the ever-present danger of having his activities develop into serious law-breaking—and became a useful member of society. Peace officers and honest citizens might have found cause to feel grateful for that. His *Nemenuh* upbringing would have made him a terrible and murderous outlaw if he had been driven to a life of violent crime.

Obtaining his first repeating rifle—a Winchester Model of 1866, although at first known as the "New Improved Henry," nicknamed the "Old Yellowboy" because of its brass frame —while in Mexico with Dusty and Mark, the Kid soon became a master in its use. At the first Cochise County Fair in Arizona, despite circumstances having compelled him to rely upon a weapon with which he was not familiar, he won the first prize in the rifle-shooting competition against stiff opposition. The prize was one of the legendary Winchester Model of 1873 rifles that qualified for the honored title "One of a Thousand."

It was, in part, through the efforts of the Kid that the majority of the Comanche bands agreed to go on reservations, following the attempts to ruin the treaty-signing ceremony at Fort Sorrel. Dusty Fog could not have found and cleared out the outlaw town of Hell without his help. Later, he played a major part in preventing a "land grab" from provoking trouble with the Comanches. To help a young man out of difficulties with a gang of confidence tricksters, he teamed up with lady outlaw Belle Starr. When he accompanied Martha "Calamity Jane" Canary to inspect a ranch she had inherited, they became involved in as dangerous a situation as either had ever faced.

Remaining at the OD Connected ranch until he, Dusty, and Mark met their deaths while on a hunting trip in Kenya at the turn of the century, his descendants continued to be connected with the Hardin, Fog, Blaze clan, and Counter family.

APPENDIX FOUR

Left an orphan almost from birth by a Waco Indian raid, from whence came the only name he knew, Waco had been raised as one of a North Texas rancher's large family. Guns were always a part of his life and his sixteenth birthday had seen him riding with the tough, "wild onion" crew of Clay Allison. Like their employer, the CA hands were notorious for their wild and occasionally dangerous behavior. Living in the company of such men, all older than himself, he had become quick to take offense and well able, eager even, to prove he could draw his revolvers with lightning speed and shoot very accurately. It seemed only a matter of time before one shoot-out too many would see him branded as a killer and fleeing from the law with a price on his head.

Fortunately for Waco and—as was the case with the Ysabel Kid—law-abiding citizens, that day did not come!

From the day that Dusty Fog saved the youngster's life, at some considerable risk to his own, a change had come for the better. Leaving Allison, with the blessing and approval of the Washita curly wolf, Waco had become a member of the OD Connected ranch's floating outfit. The other members of that elite group had treated him like a favorite younger brother and taught him many useful lessons. Instruction in bare-handed combat was given by Mark Counter. The Kid showed him how to read tracks and many other tricks of the scouting trade. From a friend who was a gambler, Frank Derringer, had come information about the way of honest and dishonest followers of his profession. However, it was from the Rio Hondo gun wizard that the most important advice had come: *when*—he already knew *how*—to shoot. Dusty had also supplied training that, helped by an inborn flair for deductive reasoning, turned him into a peace officer of exceptional merit. Benefiting from such a wide education, he became noted in law enforcement circles. Having served with the Arizona Rangers—in company with Marvin Eldridge "Doc" Leroy—and as sheriff of Two Forks County, Utah, he was eventually appointed a United States marshal.